THE NET

Sara Allegrini

THE NET

How do you save someone who doesn't want to be saved?

THE NET
By Sara Allegrini

Original Title: La Rete

Translated from Italian by: Fred Proulx III

Edited by: Suzanne Tanzi

© 2019 Mondadori Libri S.p.A., Milano

Cover:
© 2019 Mondadori Libri S.p.A., Milano

Graphic designer Stefano Moro, Shutterstock images

Copyright © 2024 Human Adventure Books
17105 Longacres Ln
Odessa, FL 33556

www.humanadventurebooks.com

ISBN: 978-1-941457-26-9

The quote from the Bible on Page 141 is taken from the 1992 CEI Edition

The quote from the Adventures of Pinocchio on Page 5 is taken from the Mondadori Edition (Oscar Junior Classics, Milan 2015)

PART ONE

DANIEL

"Get in."

He had never seen his father so serious and determined. He didn't move. He just answered him with a snarky smirk, to keep him from thinking he had won, to keep him from seeing that this new attitude rattled him.

"Get in!" his father barked in reply.

Okay, he wasn't kidding around.

Annoyed, he climbed into the car. His father placed his phone on the dashboard, far away from himself. Daniel had no intention of carrying on a conversation; he dug his cell phone out of his pocket and began tapping on the screen.

"Can you please stop it with that phone?" his father asked him after a good 10 minutes.

Daniel didn't even look up. He never did what his father told him; he never did what others told him.

The man clenched his jaw and did not say anything more. Daniel really didn't like the scowl on his face that he spied out of the corner of his eye; he had really never seen the man behaving like that. But he shrugged his shoulders and continued to tune him out anyway.

His father drove on in absolute silence for at least an hour. They made their way out of the city and passed along back roads he had never seen before.

"Can you please tell me where the hell we're going?" asked Daniel finally, tired of sitting in the car. His phone battery was dying and his friends were waiting for him at the station. He also had some stuff to pick up.

His father ignored him, giving him a taste of his own medicine.

"My old man is crazy," he texted the Hunchback. "If tomorrow I'm not in school, call the police!" and he added a string of smiles and emojis: knife, blood, skull, coffin.

His friend answered with a smiley face with tears splashing from its eyes.

After another half hour, however, he was not in the mood to joke anymore, and he began to get nervous.

"Are you going to tell me where the hell we're going?"

"Speak nicely," his father answered him mechanically.

"I'll speak as I damn well please," Daniel hammered the point home.

His father remained silent, but the scowl returned to his face and Daniel was on the brink of trying to take it off with his fist. He refrained only because he remembered what had happened at home.

The car left the main street, and after going on for a long time on the bare ground with no paved road, it stopped in a kind of glade in the middle of a forest. Daniel looked out the window; he had been messing around on his phone the whole time without really taking in his surroundings, so he didn't have any idea where they were. Even less *why* they were there.

"Give me your phone," his father said in a way that he didn't like one little bit.

"Say 'please,'" he teased, taunting him.

"Please," he added, calmly.

"No!" Daniel burst out laughing, and in reply he plunged back into the game he had left halfway through.

His father rolled down the window. Daniel heard him take a big breath of air and then exhale it all out, as if counting to 10. *Attaboy*, he thought cynically, *get a grip*. He snickered. But then suddenly and unexpectedly his father snatched the phone from his hands and hurled it violently out of the car against a large boulder. The phone tumbled to the ground like something dead.

"What the h—-"

This time his father didn't let him finish his sentence.

"Get out of the car," he ordered.

Daniel looked at his face; the glow he saw in his eyes for the first time, flashing with fury, left him speechless.

"Get out!" his father yelled at him, his face red with rage.

Without really understanding what was going on, Daniel got out of the car. His father stretched into the passenger seat and closed the door. He put the car into reverse and, without a word, without even glancing back, he drove away.

Daniel watched him pull away, his mouth wide open. What kind of prank was this? "He'll be back," he said out loud, to reassure himself. He was certain he would come back for him as soon as his temper cooled.

Yeah, but maybe this time he had screwed up a little too badly. He hadn't ever done it before; he just couldn't control himself. And he hadn't really sized up his own strength. He was used to beating up people much bigger than he was. So, his mother had gone down like a rag doll right away.

His mother was a nuisance, a ball-buster, whiny and clingy. They had just taken her right out of his hands.

And his father, as usual, had been speechless, not knowing what to do. I mean, he had called the ambulance, but then she came to her senses, nothing too serious.

Daniel shrugged; sometimes you just had to do what you had to do. Of course, now his mother would stop, once and for all, all of her bullshit about doing well in school, and not going out every afternoon, and making him come home early in the evening, and not hanging out with "the thugs," as she called them.

He went to pick up his cell phone in the grass. He cursed through clenched teeth; the screen was completely smashed and it wouldn't turn on. He had paid a fortune for it, with the money from the drugs he sold to the high school jerks. The Hunchback had ripped it off one of them and sold it to Daniel.

In any event, it was now useless, and Daniel angrily flung it back against the boulder to finish it off, like a crippled horse.

He looked around; he was in a forest. It had been ages since he'd been to one. The first and last time he'd been to such a place was maybe when he was four years old. They'd gone to collect chestnuts and for a solid 10 minutes, which felt like a lifetime, he'd lost track of his parents and found himself alone, frozen stiff. Those minutes were pure terror; he was sure he'd been abandoned there. Then he screamed, he called out for his mother, and his voice echoed in agonizing silence.

She came out of nowhere, smiling as if nothing had happened. The memory of that day sent a chill down his spine, even all these years later, and for a moment Daniel felt exactly as he did then. He hated the woods, he decided. It was a horrible place; he was a jungle animal, okay, but of the asphalt kind.

He sat on the boulder with his legs crossed, lowering his hat over his eyes. There was nothing left for him to do but wait for his father to come back for him. He didn't doubt for a second that he would. He just had to keep his cool and stay calm. He grabbed his tobacco pouch and wrappers and started rolling a cigarette. He smoked in a relaxed way, with his eyes closed, enjoying the unfamiliar silence of the place. It felt good, all in all, now that he wasn't a kid anymore and wasn't scared of certain things. He had never been like that in his whole life; alone in the silence, with no cell phone in his hand and nothing to do.

He waited. And he waited. He strained to hear the far-off sound of the engine of his father's beat-up car coming closer. His earlier behavior was unlike him; he was typically weak, a coward.

He didn't know how much time had passed; his phone was busted, and he'd left his watch at home. He'd "borrowed" that as well, let's say, from a schoolmate younger than he was who'd chickened out and didn't put up a fight. Maybe an hour, maybe two; time seemed to run differently in that place. This began to put him on edge quite a bit. The sky was changing color. He didn't look up often, but he seemed to remember, as he left the house, a clearer sky than it was now.

Dusk was falling and there wasn't even a trace of his father. He got up from the boulder and took a few steps around. Even if he wanted to, he realized, he would never make it home. He hadn't been paying attention to the route, and he didn't have any idea where he was. The trees and directions all seemed the same. He couldn't even find the tire tracks on the ground. Maybe if there had been at least one road, he would have taken it and walked somewhere. But like this... He thought. Leaving the glade might turn out to be a bad idea. If he left, his father wouldn't find him when he came to pick him up. He was sure he would ... tomorrow.

He was reminded of a story the teacher had told him in kindergarten, about two little brothers abandoned in the woods by their parents. When she told the story, the chestnut fiasco had already happened to him, and hearing the teacher talk about it had literally shocked him. "Parents don't abandon their children in the woods," she reassured him, noticing his expression.

And yet, now it was happening to him. Crazy, even if he was no longer a little child.

When night fell, Daniel started to be seriously afraid.

With no moon, the darkness was total. Daniel stood with his eyes open and could see nothing, as if his eyelids were closed. That was no ordinary darkness. It was thick and clammy, and it had icy fingers that he imagined could grasp him at any moment. It was a pulsating darkness, coming closer, enveloping him and withdrawing, leaving him covered in a cold sweat. It was alive and evil. And it wanted him dead.

Then there were the noises: on the ground, under the ground, and in the trees overhead. Rustling everywhere, snapping and crunching in the foliage, a trampling of unknown and unseen paws. Half-human shrieks rose suddenly from the darkness, and then grunts, choked breathing, a beast lurking in the shadows, another sneaking closer, sniffing greedily, then padding away. A little farther on, too close for comfort, there was the dull sound of a body being beaten, falling to the ground, something else grabbing it, shaking it, strangling it, and then eating it, carving its way through the hot entrails with its teeth.

Those noises rang in Daniel's ears loudly, as if he had Superman's hearing. He knew it was terror playing tricks on him, but he couldn't escape it. All that hearing without being able to see put his imagination into overdrive, making him picture the most horrible things. By now, he was on the brink of insanity. Eventually, a terrible, almost human sigh arose from the darkness; in a few seconds, the thought seized him that a corpse had been buried out there somewhere and was now rising up to get him. He cowered in his jacket, shaking with fright.

The cold descended at last. It was damp and there was a moment when Daniel sincerely thought he was going to die, the temperature had fallen so low. His teeth were chattering and he tried to stretch his jacket out on all sides, but when he covered his legs, his neck was freezing, and vice versa. He got it into his head that a mouse was gnawing at his feet, which had lost all feeling. So with his hands he was constantly checking that he still had his shoes on and that there were no holes for some animal to creep through and eat him. He had heard stories of babies being eaten in their sleep by mice, and the parents finding them dead in their cribs. Ugh, why were all these stories coming back to him *now*? And why on earth had they been told to him, anyway? Part of him knew that the fear of being devoured piece by piece was stupid, but in the darkness, surrounded by those noises, the dread made anything seem believable. He had never thought the night could be like this. He wanted and needed to stay awake, even though his eyes were tearing up with the cold, exhausted from staring into the dark.

And yet, at one point, they closed on him; when he opened them again in fright, it seemed like only an instant had passed. He looked around, sightless. He was absolutely sure, though he could not make it out, that there was someone very close by. He could sense him, someone who could see him perfectly, who was watching him, but whom he could not pinpoint in the darkness. He could only hear his breath, slow and controlled, very close to him.

"Who's there?" he shouted, trying to put an edge of aggression in his voice, to keep it from shaking, but the humidity and the lingering silence brought out a kind of wheezing that scared even him. It didn't even sound like his own voice to him.

No one answered. He covered his ears with his hands and buried his head between his legs. He had a feeling that, at any moment, someone was going to hit him with a hatchet, or pierce him through with a knife. He had seen too many horror films and now they were coming back to him all at once. He wanted to scream, but he had no voice. And who would hear him anyway? Who would rush to his aid? Someone wanted to kill him, in the dark, and all he could do was sit there, waiting to feel the sudden pain of the blade between his ribs. It was all a nightmare. It had to be. He couldn't wake up, though. What was he doing there? Maybe this is how people go crazy.

When he revived from those long minutes of sheer terror, he was sure, without knowing how, that the presence was gone. He breathed deeply, once, twice; each breath of icy air into his lungs was like the first breath of an infant. It seemed to him that he had been in a state of breathlessness all that time. His heart slowed, and Daniel forced himself to control his shaking.

After what had seemed an endless night, he noticed with relief the sky beginning to lighten. The silhouettes of the trees slowly came into focus before his eyes, at first surreal, then increasingly familiar and calming. As the light returned, the fears faded and all appeared in their absurdity. Knives, rats, madness, death; what an idiot he had been!

He searched his pockets for the tobacco and painstakingly rolled a cigarette, his fingers trembling and frozen. He lit it to warm himself and feel that he was still alive. When he had the lighter in his hand, he burst out laughing hysterically, taunting himself. Why on earth had he not used it to light a fire? It hadn't even crossed his mind, dimwit that he was! The truth was that he had never used a lighter to do anything. For cigarettes, of course, and once he had even set fire to a class assignment; it was too difficult, he had told the teacher who stared at him in astonishment. *I'm such a dummy.* He brushed the whole thing off. If his friends had seen him in that state, he would have never heard the end of it.

Then he lowered his eyes and felt he would have a heart attack.

At the foot of the same boulder that the mobile phone had smashed against was a folded sheet of paper. He trembled. At that moment he understood: during the night, someone had gotten close enough to put it right under his nose.

He looked around, then bent down and picked it up. It was a map. He turned the paper over in his hands, not quite knowing what to do with it. It was clear that somebody, who did not want to be known, was asking him to go somewhere. And also that person was in cahoots with his father. There was no way this could have been a coincidence. It was all so strange that it might have been a dream, except for the hunger, thirst, and cold, which were all too real. How many hours had it been since he had eaten something? He used to eat a lot in school and had suffered a considerable amount of stern warnings about it! Chips, sandwiches, croissants, soft drinks. . . His mouth immediately began to water.

He spat on the ground and went back to looking at the map. From the red arrow on the map, it was clear that he had to go north, if only he could figure out where the hell he was. He vaguely remembered hearing about compass directions in school. Not for nothing, it was his third time repeating the last year of high school. But he had never believed that something taught in school could really be of any use in life. He wandered in the woods for a while, feeling like a complete fool. So he kicked a tree in aggravation, but only hurt himself and broke one of his boots, which opened like a duck's beak. It was just ludicrous! What the hell was going on? Why on earth had his father dumped him here? And where was "here"? He crumpled up the map and shoved it in his pocket. He didn't want to give in to his father or whoever the bastard was who was toying with him.

Then another story from kindergarten popped into his memory: the little boy who scattered stones in order to find his way home. And that was what he began doing, marking the woods with signs so he could always turn back, even though he was beginning to despair that his father would come back for him. He had even tried to climb a tree; maybe from up high he could find a way out of this crazy situation. But instead he had scraped his hands, torn his pants, and realized that his arms were not strong enough, especially since he had a sickening hunger twisting in his stomach and a wicked thirst. For the first time in his life, he felt a great urge to cry, but he wouldn't give the satisfaction to anyone who was watching him. Because even though he couldn't see it, he felt a cold stare on him.

"The sun sets in the west!" he suddenly remembered, when he was no longer thinking about it. For a moment he felt smart. But then was the north ahead or behind his back? And immediately he called himself an idiot again. Anyway, just in case, he stacked some stones in a mound to remind himself the next day, at least, which was west. Meanwhile, the sun had set. Hopelessness dropped on his shoulders like a sack of concrete. He huddled at the foot of the boulder and prepared to face the second night.

He gathered as much wood as he could and tried to set it on fire with a lighter, but it didn't work; it was too damp and rotten. He tried with leaves and immediately the smoke completely enveloped him and burned his throat, making him even more thirsty. After half an hour of trying, a small, timid fire started to catch. He felt uplifted by this paltry success. He would have gladly thrown in the map as well, but it was probably his only chance for rescue. He prayed with all the profanities he knew, and without realizing it, late at night, he dozed off.

There were strange creatures hovering around him, crawling and stretching their long necks to see him better. Their faces had no expression. They were whispering and laughing at him, laughing that he was clueless.

He woke up with his heart beating wildly. The fire had gone out. He clicked the lighter; there was no one there. He froze. Next to him he found two items: a small bottle of water and a compass. He drank it all at once. The water ran out too soon; Daniel crumpled the bottle and threw it far away. The cold had entered through the gash in his shoe. It seemed to him that it, too, was laughing at him. His foot was practically frozen. This time the rats could have really chewed it off and he wouldn't have even noticed. He stuffed some dried leaves into the hole, blew on the embers, added a few twigs, and waited for the day, his teeth chattering.

When dawn came, bright and warm, Daniel felt as if he was outside of himself, almost like he was another person. He hadn't been there even two days, but the world from before seemed so far away to him, in time and space. Maybe he had ended up in a movie or some stupid reality show, because the plot line was unbelievable. What had happened to his people? And why was no one coming for him? How much longer could he last in these conditions?

There was gurgling in his empty stomach. He felt seized by a nameless grief. He also stank, ached all over, and it was as if ice filled his insides, completely replacing his bones. He seemed to have forgotten how to speak. So he began to talk to himself, out loud, like crazy people do.

"All right, Daniel," he opened the map. "Let's figure this out."

He began walking in the marked direction, looking at the compass. It took all morning to figure it out, but as he went along, he recognized landmarks and felt proud of himself. It was the first time in his life that he had faced a difficult situation alone. He cursed through his teeth, his tongue sticking to his palate. Couldn't the bastard who left me water also give me a sandwich? At the thought of food he felt his legs start to give out and his mouth go dry. He was getting closer to the point of arrival marked on the map. What would he find?

He was feeling almost sick when, among the trees, he spotted a shed. It was a sagging shack, but for someone who had been roughing it for two nights, it was like a Hilton suite. He hurried, threw open the door, and was inside. The inside was no better: a dirty, smelly cubbyhole. A good den for a bum, not for him. The floor was uneven and creaked loudly with every movement. Probably, he imagined, at any moment it would open up like a chasm under his feet.

He punched the wooden wall, but it didn't move; at least it seemed to be holding up, even if the planks were not perfectly connected and would certainly let the frigid air and the sounds of the woods through. There was a gross mattress thrown on the floor, lumpy and stained yellow, with a folded blanket being the most that those who had thrown it there had managed to gather. On the opposite side of the room was some kind of rusty, broken-down stove in which, from the looks of it, you would have guessed had burned a few acres of forest. In one corner, someone had left a bucket. Daniel was horrified; it was for bathroom needs, he concluded from the smell. He picked it up and threw it out; he would never do it in a bucket, that was for sure. He searched every nook and cranny, but found no food. He was sure that by now he would have devoured even the wood of the forest as long as he could put something in his belly. Hanging on the wall, he noticed a slingshot. He went out again and looked for some animals to target. The forest was full of birds, but apparently they were much smarter than he was and fled as soon as he took half a step. He had no idea it was so difficult to shoot with a slingshot! It was the second day completely on an empty stomach; how long could you go without food before dying? Now *this* was an interesting thing they should have taught in school: how to survive alone in the middle of nowhere, without a cell phone, with a compass and a lighter.

He struggled to light the stove, which, although destroyed, did its job. Then he threw himself on the bed and fell fast asleep.

He awoke in the morning with a backache that could top the Guinness world record. The mattress had confirmed what it promised at first glance. The blanket, on the other hand, had kept him warm, and he had slept so soundly in his exhaustion that he did not even notice the noises outside. After all, those four wooden walls, thin as they were, had made him feel safe. He stretched like a cat and jerked when he noticed what was beside him on the floor. He could not believe his eyes; it was a can of chickpeas.

Chickpeas were the food he hated most in the world, because of their smell and texture. However, considering the circumstances, he could not be so picky; he would have eaten a snake. He opened the can and gobbled them down, fishing from the bottom with his fingers and drinking every last drop of their salty water. Once, he remembered, he had thrown a plate of chickpea pasta his mother had made for him on the floor. Now, he would have given his mother away to have one more forkful. In any case, chickpeas were disgusting, but they were certainly better than nothing.

His stomach was more or less settled, but something else caught his attention. Attached to the wall was a white sheet of paper with black writing, sharply clear.

TAKE AWAY THE STONES FROM THE FIELD,
PLEASE.

What field? thought Daniel. He walked out of the hut with a bad feeling. An area about the size of a soccer field had been cordoned off in the night with stakes and red and white tape. It looked like a crime scene; only the corpse was missing. He took two more steps. Leaning against the back of the shack was a hoe. Was he supposed to use that contraption? And *this* was the field?! *If I catch the bastard who put me here*, he thought, sneering to himself, *there really will be a corpse. And I'll use the hoe to bury the body, besides digging up stones.* He talked to himself, muttering and threatening, but the only certainty was his helplessness. Besides cursing and lashing out at the invisible man, what else could he do? There was no face to slap and spit at, there was nothing to break or kick in that shitty place! However, one thing was sure: in his life, he had never obeyed anyone, and he certainly wasn't going to start now, much less to please someone who wasn't even showing his face and for something as meaningless as taking rocks out of a soccer field.

He went back inside the shed, looked around, and then, congratulating himself on his ingenuity, took a piece of charred wood from the stove and wrote angrily on the back of the paper:

I'M HUNGRY

Then he threw himself on the mattress, determined not to move a finger. In the past, he had spent whole days sleeping, waking up only to eat. No problem.

He shoved a hand into his pocket and there he had his second unpleasant surprise. While he was sleeping, the bastard must have taken away his lighter and tobacco. How on earth had he missed him? Maybe he was dealing with a spirit, like in a horror movie. He shuddered.

In that forsaken place, even the craziest things could happen for real. He didn't like being afraid. If anything, he was the one who had always made others afraid.

He cursed again. And again. He was helpless and brimming with anger. He wished he had someone there to beat up, wringing his hands to calm his nerves. And if that weren't enough, it was beginning to get cold. He checked the stove and there was only one tiny ember still burning. He spent almost an hour struggling to get his fire back. He went out to gather more wood and scattered it on the floor to let it dry out a bit. The fire eventually recovered. "Daniel 1, Bastard 0!" he shouted against the ceiling, hoping someone would hear him.

At the doorway, with the sun now setting, he looked around one last time to see if there was anything to bite into. He found nothing at all and went to sleep, furious. If he could have, he would have barred the doorway to prevent the bastard from entering, but there was nothing to use, short of moving the mattress in front of the door, exposing himself to all the drafts. On the floor again, he couldn't sleep soundly. *Drop dead*, was his last thought before falling asleep.

The next day, he opened his eyes as the sun was rising. Never in his life had he woken up so early. He was shivering and dragged himself to the stove to rekindle the fire once more. He felt weak; he absolutely had to find something to eat. With his vision vaguely blurred, he noticed that while he slept the paper on the wall had been replaced. "I'm hungry," he had written. And now the sheet read:

HE WHO DOES NOT WORK, DOES NOT EAT.
REMOVE THE STONES FROM THE FIELD,
PLEASE.

Daniel felt his anger mounting. That was blackmail good and proper. You can't force people to do something by starving them. He went out to see if at least the field had been made smaller. Hopefully, seeing that he couldn't handle it . . .

Everything was the same as before. Next to the hoe, there was now a bottle of water and some kind of red salad. Daniel never ate vegetables, but that morning he wasn't picky. Without even washing it, so as not to waste water and time, he ate half the salad. It crunched under his teeth and was bitter as hell, but at least it was edible. The bastard must have had a wicked irony, starving him by foisting on him everything he hated most. Surely he had been well informed about him, about his tastes, which, by the way, meant that fish would be next, the second thing he hated most after chickpeas.

He took the hoe and listlessly began to work. The soil was hard and full of stones, so it was clear that the request to hoe it was a provocation. He went on sluggishly for about twenty minutes, then the wooden handle began to bother his hands and he threw it on the ground in a huff. He would get blisters the size of walnuts and he hadn't even covered one square yard of soil. When he lifted one stone, there was always another one underneath. It's totally useless busywork; it can't be done, he reasoned to himself, and gave up.

He let the rest of the day slip away in boredom. He tried a few half-hearted launches with the slingshot, hitting tree trunks. He gathered more wood and finished the gross salad. He had a hard time getting to sleep, out of hunger and resentment. His blood was boiling, and he continued to curse his father and the unknown bastard. At the moment, he had no idea how to get out of it but, without a doubt, once he was out of that nightmare, he was going to make them pay, all of them. He would report them and have them thrown in jail, at the very least. He fell asleep on a half-empty stomach, savoring the taste of that imagined revenge.

When he woke up the next morning, Daniel immediately ran his eyes to the wall. The sign had not been changed; the words were the same as the day before. He went out to see what the bastard had left for him to eat this time. Next to the hoe there was nothing, neither water nor food. He was disappointed; who knows why, he didn't really expect any food. But the message was clear: no work, no food. He imagined his jailor secretly watching him and laughing. Choking back anger, he grabbed the hoe and began the pointless endeavor again. With each swing, an expletive. It was like he was drunk with frustration and went on for quite a while, head down, almost without feeling hunger or fatigue anymore. With each swing he imagined hitting the bastard who was making fun of him in cahoots with his father.

After several hours of futile work, he sat on the ground, out of breath. He looked at the pile of stones he had quarried from the field and was surprised to see that it was very large. His nails were black and broken, his palms were blistered, his back was screaming, and his temples were sweaty and throbbing. He stank to high heaven. An overwhelming thirst clung to his throat and the fierce bite of hunger in his belly returned.

He dragged himself to the shack with the intention of sleeping for two whole days; he had never worked so hard in his life. On the ground next to the stove, he found a new can of chickpeas, with the usual bottle of water, always insufficient, and a piece of old bread. Next to it, a bucket with water and blue overalls. He was surprised, first of all, that the man had once again come so close to him without being heard or seen in any way. How had he managed to carry that bucket, without a clue that he'd been there? He threw his dirty clothes into a corner, washed his hands, face, and body, drying himself, shivering all over in the meager heat of the stove. Sitting cross-legged on the floor, he devoured that simple meal, which a few days earlier he would have thrown in the face of anyone who had offered it to him. He dipped the dry bread in the chickpea water, so as not to break a tooth and give it some flavor. It still sucked, but he was not going to let that situation break him. Even though it was still light outside, he decided that he had done enough hard work for the day. He felt like a wreck and it didn't take more than three seconds to fall asleep.

That night, his confidence began to waver. Already earlier, in the afternoon, he had begun to feel strange. He had eaten very little and poorly and worked far too much. And then all that sweat had frozen on him and after having washed himself with cold water, in front of a half-lit stove. . . He felt feverish. At first it was a mild discomfort, his head heavy, his legs weak. But then he began to shiver, his teeth chattering. He wasn't a doctor and he didn't have a thermometer, but he didn't need either to know that his head was pounding and his forehead was hot. *The last time I was sick I was in middle school*, he thought. He had caught a virus and even passed out in the bathroom. His mother had pampered him like a prince, had even spoon-fed him. He had cussed her out, first because he didn't feel well, and then because he was better and her attention was getting on his nerves. Yes, his mother was definitely too clingy. He wished she could have been there with him now, though, because he felt so sick and was terrified he would pass out and stay for hours on the cold floor, freezing to death without anyone knowing anything about it. There was no medicine, and maybe the bastard didn't even know that he was unwell.

Even though he lacked strength, he forced himself to go out and get wood for the stove. Then he had to give in and take the piss pot inside; he would not be able to get out, as he had done the other days. When he felt he was about to faint, he closed the door and threw himself on the mattress with his jacket and shoes still on. The blanket was not enough to keep him warm.

He woke up in the middle of the night screaming from a nightmare. He had dug a huge hole with his hoe and got into it, and then the earth had started to cave in on him and he was screaming, but there was no one there who could hear him. The earth had gotten into his mouth and he felt like he was suffocating. With the sensation of running out of air and being buried alive, he found himself sitting up on the mattress. He opened and closed his eyes and waited for the room to stop spinning; the fire in the stove had been rekindled and on the floor was a metal box with a spoon and a round tablet beside it. The tablet stood out against the blackness of the floor like a button. Daniel reached out his hand and saw that it was shaking. Then he took the metal container and it was boiling hot. He warmed his icy hands on it; he took off his shoes and warmed his feet as well. Then he opened the lid and a hospital smell invaded his nostrils. Just broth and noodles, yet it seemed to him that there was nothing more desirable and good at that moment. He drank it, slowly, with difficulty, still feeling like he had a clump of dirt in his throat. The warmth of the soup loosened his stomach and relaxed him. With the rest of the broth he downed the tablet. Don't think I'm thanking you, he said mentally to the bastard; it's your fault I'm like this. He threw himself back to sleep without being able to control the trembling that the fever put on him.

In the morning, he woke up late, totally sweaty. He thought he would find more hot food for breakfast, but instead there was nothing at all. Without knowing why, he felt like crying. He was fucking sick! Why was no one coming to help him? He bet it was illegal to treat people this way. He sat up on the mattress, feeling totally broken. The sign was always there, always the same, giving him orders. He decided he would not lift a finger that day. It was not right, and whoever had put him there had to give him more food, because he did not have the strength to do anything. He went back to sleep. For lunch, maybe something to eat would appear.

His stomach told him that mealtime must have come and gone. First, it started to grumble, then it twisted around like there was a snake in his belly. There was nothing on the floor. At least he felt a little better. He got up from the mattress and peeked outside, to see if maybe there was something next to the shed. Not a chance! He should have known better. Livid with anger he picked up his hoe and started digging again. It's impossible, he told himself, biting his lip; it's impossible. But, in the meantime, he dug.

He went back into the shack in a wretched state. He stank, but he did not have the will to take off his dirty overalls and wash himself. In front of the unlit stove, the usual can of chickpeas. *This guy has no imagination*, he thought. Neither does he have an ounce of mercy – although Daniel didn't ever want pity from anyone. On the contrary, he had even once brought his fist rather close to the face of a teacher who had looked at him in a way he did not appreciate at all. *Anyway*, he thought despondently, *if he were home, his mother would have prepared him a 16-ounce steak cooked rare, to regain his strength after the fever, with a nice side of french fries and ketchup. . .* He gave himself a smack on his head, because just the thought of that meal made his stomach give a tug, simultaneously making his other hand lose its grip on the can, which fell on his foot. For a second, the pain made him see stars. Why on earth had he taken off his shoes? He checked to confirm that his toe was still attached to his foot; from the pain it felt as if the can had cut it off. He pulled the sock off; the toe was still there, throbbing. It had hit him right in the middle. *The nail would turn black and then fall off,* he thought; it had happened to his father once. He shuddered in disgust. He pressed his toe with his hands, as if this would drive away the pain, but it didn't work. He had run out of swear words, too. This latest catastrophe, even though it was no big thing, brought his spirits down. He felt like crying again, from the pain, the hunger, the exhaustion, the feeling of being in a dead-end dilemma. He swallowed a few times to chase back the tears. There was no one who could see him, it was true, but he knew he should not cry for himself, because it would mean that he was throwing in the towel, that he was giving in to the blackmail of the bastard who kept him there, that he would not make it through, to see the end of this insane story. "See, I told you that chickpeas are bad for you," he said to himself aloud, and even managed to make himself laugh. He opened the dented can and ate that slop slowly, until he felt sick to his stomach. It was disgusting, disgusting, and still more disgusting.

He lost count of the days. The toenail had turned black, as expected, and this had been the only thrilling change in his days, days that were all identical. He could feel it, though he didn't want to tell himself: he was getting discouraged. Perhaps he should have at least tried, at first, to get out of the woods. Now it was too late; he would never have the strength. Faintly, he continued to pile up stones, hour after hour. It made no sense, but he had to do it if he didn't want to starve to death. Where had his parents gone? Could it be that they did not care about him at all? He sat on the pile of stones with his head in his hands, without a thought, totally drained.

That evening, in the shack, he found a large piece of bread besides the chickpeas. It was not the usual smashed, old, dried-up lump; this one was fresh and smelled of flour and a wood-burning oven. He took it in his hands like something he had never seen, broke it and the crunchy sound of the crust made his mouth fill with saliva. He remembered when, as a child, he went with his mother to the bakery. When they left the shop and got on the street, holding his hand, she would tear off a piece of freshly baked bread and feed it to him immediately, winking at him complicitly as if they were doing something forbidden. He tore off the first piece with a bite and chewed it greedily. Bread had never seemed so good to him; in fact, it seemed to him that he was really tasting it for the first time. WTF — what were those thoughts? Bread was bread, fine. Yet, for a moment, he felt like he was home. It was only a fleeting sensation, but after all the fatigue and exhaustion of those days, putting something fresh and good in his mouth gave him unexpected courage. It was totally absurd, but it occurred to him that there was even something beautiful about sitting there, staring into the fire, chewing on fresh bread with his clean clothes on and his body, broken by fatigue, finally resting. It wasn't the pace of a life that could be kept up forever but, he told himself, he had never been one to make plans for the future. It'll be as long at it'll be. He couldn't get out of there but in the end, after all is said and done, the main thing was to have something decent to put in his stomach, because hunger was the worst thing he had experienced up to that point.

He lay down on the bed and slept as deeply as he could ever remember sleeping in his entire life.

For another week, he continued to quarry stones from morning to night, eat the bland, lukewarm chickpeas twice a day, and doing his business inside a bucket. Several times he had tried to catch the mystery man red-handed, but he had never succeeded, and maybe he didn't even care after all. He missed the cigarettes and the reassuring presence of the cell phone, but after the first few days of abstinence, he had almost come to terms with it. More to the point, how could his parents go so long without knowing anything about him, if they really loved him as much as they said they did? What about his friends? Hadn't the Hunchback become suspicious, having neither seen nor heard from him for days? Maybe he had already replaced him. Who knows what the hell was going on outside that forest. If he told his story, no one would have believed it. My old man abandoned me in a forest. I slept two nights outside, then found a shack and dug rocks out of the ground for weeks, eating stuff that appeared from out of nowhere, and peeing in a bucket.

It was the stupidest thing the world had ever heard of.

When the field was completely free of stones, a new sign appeared.

THANK YOU. GOOD WORK.

TILL THE GROUND, PLEASE.

Daniel had no idea what the word "till" meant but, more than anything else, the first sentence struck him. In 17 years no one had ever told him that he had done a great job. He felt pleased with himself, even though he had no idea who the stranger was, who was assigning him these stupid jobs, and what his purpose was. To him it was pointless labor; it was equivalent to studying history or grammar. No, not geography, he half reconsidered; he had realized, at his own expense, that maybe that was a reasonable pursuit. *And, in any case, what do I care what someone I don't even know says?* he repeated to himself. So he hurled all the curses he could at him, lambasted him with all the nastiest words he knew, and finally wished him death in the most painful of ways. It was a matter of pride; he could not admit, not even for a moment, that he might care even a little about his judgment and that in reading those words he had felt a sort of pleasure.

As the days passed, the food also changed. There was often fish beside the stove, as expected. But it was nothing like what his mother used to serve at home. It was not stick-shaped. This was fish-fish, almost alive, or just dead, which is basically the same. The first time, shivering with disgust, he had tried cooking it on the stove as it was, touching it as little as possible. It was disgusting: the innards were bitter and had made everything else inedible. Then, out of necessity, he had taken courage and with a sharp stone he had opened its belly and emptied it of everything. A revolting endeavor, but that time at least the result had been edible, although he still disliked the taste of the fish and it smelled too strongly, in his mouth and on his fingers.

He still did not know what "tilling" meant, but he had no intention of asking. Asking meant admitting he needed help, and there was no question of doing *that*. It was one thing to agree to work in order to survive and eat; it was another to stoop to ask. Only the weak ask, he told himself; the strong take without asking. So he reasoned and finally put two and two together. He had cleared a rectangle of land of stones and had received no tools other than the usual hoe. He couldn't be sure, but maybe the guy intended to make his own private vegetable garden in the woods, inside that little patch of earth. There were some strange people out there. He took his hoe and with that he set out to slay the soil, breaking it up and turning over the clods. It was a good way to keep from being strangled by the anger that at certain times was eating him up from within.

"I guess I got it right," he said to himself encouragingly after a few days. The stranger had evidently found nothing to complain about and had continued to provide him with food, even a tad more plentiful than usual.

How long had he been there? He had long since lost count of the days. And what was the point of continuing to speculate about it anyway? In any case, it was clear that no one would come looking for him. At least not for the time being. Everyone seemed to have forgotten about him. Sometimes the loneliness became unbearable, especially at night, when he was overwhelmed by the mysterious silence of the forest and felt like the last person on earth. One morning, however, a beautiful thing happened to him. A creature came to keep him company.

On top of the pile of his garbage, a cat was scraping. It was not a beautiful animal; it was missing an eye and had a mangled ear and sparse red fur. It was probably the ugliest and most flea-ridden cat in the world.

"Here kitty. . ." he called softly, afraid it would run away.

The cat didn't run away, and Daniel was even able to pet him. The warmth of the fur under his fingers, the movement of the small bones, gave him a strange feeling he had never experienced before. He had never had a pet; in fact, he had never even wanted one. He would have had to take care of it, and he didn't have the time, with all he had to do. But in the undefined and silent vastness of the forest, that cat seemed to him as beautiful as anything that could happen to him and made him feel less lonely. Eventually, he named him Kitty. He had never had much imagination.

Kitty was a good friend; he watched him work, but not with the haughty expression that cats usually have. Daniel felt that he understood his fatigue. He kept him company while he ate, and he nuzzled up against him to get his end of the bargain. Even though he was ugly and gaunt, he cared a great deal about hygiene and with perhaps excessive care licked his paws and raked his ears. It put Daniel in a good mood, that scrappy cat. Of course, they would never choose him to make Kibble commercials, Daniel chuckled to himself but, to him, he was the most beautiful beast in the world. He kept him entertained and, in his own way, feeling loved, as an animal who considers you his master can do. In any case, Kitty was an independent animal; to Daniel, he seemed the right pet for him. In an impossible and mysterious way, they were alike.

He caressed him on the head with his rough hand, and the cat closed its eyes and went along with it by nuzzling up against him. In bed that night, he curled up on his belly and Daniel fell asleep watching the cat's chest rise and fall with his own breath.

Tilling the soccer field, as he called it, probably took a few centuries. By now his body had caught up with the rhythm of the sun; he would open his eyes as soon as the sky became clear, calmly give himself a wash, and warm his milk in the metal cup, a pleasant novelty that had been added since he had started tilling. He would have a chat with Kitty and then go out to work. He would continue with his head down until the sun came straight over his head, then he would stop, because he knew that lunch must have appeared. He still could not explain how the stranger was never seen, but he had stopped trying to catch him, because the two or three times he had made the effort he had run out of food. In the end, he told himself, what did he care about seeing his face?

After lunch, he would take a break, either lying on his mattress or wandering around with Kitty. The woods were beginning to look familiar to him, but still he was pretty far from liking them. He had the impression that the forest hid something ominous, although during the day it was almost beautiful, with its colors and the birds fluttering overhead as he passed. He had left the sling-shot hanging on the nail. Assuming he ever managed to hit a bird, he wouldn't have had the courage to pluck its feathers and cook it on a spit. He already struggled with fish; with birds it would be even worse.

In the afternoon, he resumed hoeing, but with less eagerness; his body was tired. When the sky turned pink and orange, Daniel began to feel lightheaded, but he went on a little longer, because he had begun a kind of challenge with himself. Every day, he took himself a little beyond the limit of his strength, to see if he could hold on and how far he could push himself. He felt that he had become strong and resilient, able to endure fatigue. He could also see it in the way his arms had changed; he liked them much better, so muscular. He imagined that, when he was able to get out of the woods, girls would be lining up to grab him.

In the evening, he would put down his hoe, go to wash, and slip into his clean clothes. It was like changing his skin.

He'd eat dinner, listlessly chase some silly thought, and pet the cat until his eyes closed on their own.

EXCELLENT WORK, THANK YOU.
PLANTING, PLEASE.

How long had the new sign been there? Impossible to say. Daniel walked out of the house, followed by Kitty.

Behind the shack, he found a series of plastic containers with plants in them. He had no idea what the stuff was. There was also a drawing, so he could understand how the work had to be done; you had to dig and place the plants at a distance of a palm and a half. *They leave me the drawing because they assume I'm an imbecile who can't make a hole in the ground and stick a plant in it,* he thought.

By now, he marveled, it came naturally to him to follow orders without asking why and wherefore. Especially since there was no one to ask questions and be controversial with. He did not know how to return home, and anyway it was obvious that no one cared about him. Why would he go back there, anyway? Being there or elsewhere was the same thing, after all, with the difference being that where he was now, paradoxically, was less tiring than at home, what with school, fights with his parents, and the struggle to maintain a high reputation in his group of friends and among strangers. Life was a long and exhausting war, and there were many battles to be fought every day. In the woods, however, Daniel felt himself in a kind of respite and agreed with himself that every now and then a break was needed.

He threw a liver to Kitty, who devoured it in that funny way of his and then came over to thank him, rubbing himself against his muddy boots. Daniel stared at the broken boot which was currently held together by a piece of wood and some string he had found in the shack. He took great pride in that ingenious repair. Kitty cleaned his paws with his tongue and looked at him gratefully. Daniel smiled: he was a polite cat.

"Good Kitty."

"Meow," he replied.

"You're welcome."

MAGDALENA

She squinted her eyes, peered at the ceiling, and immediately closed them again. She told herself that she was
probably still dreaming. She focused on the noises and
did not hear what she would have expected. She opened
her eyes again to check. Yes, what was above her head
was definitely an ugly wooden plank ceiling. Unusual.
She struggled to sit up and looked around, frowning.
The only sign of life was a lit stove heating that too-
small room, and nothing else. She threw herself back
down, her forehead furrowed in an effort to remember
how she had ended up there. She recaptured in her
mind the last memories in her possession.

Like every Friday, she had told her parents that she
was going to sleep over at Eliza's. Instead, they had gone
dancing at the usual place until four in the morning,
when they had taken the bus downtown. There they had
wandered in the cold for two hours, waiting for a café to
open for breakfast. Then she was sure she had arrived
at school; she remembered vividly the English teacher's
comment that she looked terrible. And the disapprov-
ing looks from her classmates. Then, nothing more. Of
what had happened after that she had no memory. So
why was she surprised to find a wooden ceiling over
her head? What was she supposed to see, where was she
supposed to be? At the moment, her memory and brain
were disconnected. She closed her eyes once more and

strained to fish out more details. She remembered, as if it were a dream, the smell and heat of the hospital, and with almost complete clarity the beeping of the machines near her. She had to have been there, in the hospital, but when and for how long? What day was it, and how many had passed since Friday?

She sank back into a kind of drowsiness, and dreamed of nothing. She didn't feel anything except the dark sensation clinging to her that something was wrong with her body. She felt like she was on a journey through her veins; she perceived, as if standing inside them, strange noises of moving fluids, digestive tubes, bowels writhing like snakes. It must have been the hangover from the pill she had downed in the club, along with a few too many drinks. The feeling was just that, familiar and unpleasant, of not seeming to belong to herself anymore, along with the total impossibility of putting an end to all of it. With her senses sharpened, it seemed as if the upside-down and distorted reality was bombarding her brain. Her head was spinning in circles, unable to process and comprehend. Her heart was now accelerating out of control. It felt like it was going to burst. Darkness.

She woke up covered in a cold sweat. Through the haze in front of her eyes, she still saw the wooden plank ceiling. She had not been dreaming then; this was reality. What was happening? What had they done to her? She felt like crying. She was short of breath and her body was unresponsive; it seemed to be made of stone. She had no voice in her throat to call out, no thread of strength to lift herself from that ugly bed and leave. But to call whom, then? And to go where?

She could not think; she was exhausted, consumed from within. She fell asleep again, and in her slumber she had a kind of dream, or perhaps it was a new memory surfacing, finally shedding light on the present. She was once again in the hospital, awake in bed. However, she kept her eyes closed, because she did not want anyone to notice that she was listening. She was terrified of questions, which would surely come sooner or later. Grown-ups always wanted to know everything, and usually it was the kind of "everything" that could not be told because they considered it wrong. She was not very good at lying, at least on certain topics and in certain situations. She could very well tell her mother that she was going to the library to study and instead spend the afternoon in her boyfriend's bed. However, if things got bad, such as now when she was weak between the rough hospital sheets, she could not look her father in the face and deny that she had taken a pill.

And now things were bad, because she could hear someone crying, and although she could not see her, she recognized that it was her mom. Around the corner, there where the door to the room was supposed to be, some people were talking. One was indeed her mother, crying. Magdalena could sense her despair from the sobs stifled in her handkerchief. The one speaking was a man, probably a doctor. He had a nice, young voice, but the tone was too serious and definitely bothered her.

"Are you sure?" asked the stranger in his serious way.

"Her teacher, Mrs. Speranza, explained everything to us," came her father's voice.

Mrs. Speranza was her Italian teacher. Magdalena often wondered how she, who seemed intelligent, could work for years in that kind of exclusive high school, where mommy's boys went with their beautiful futures already all planned out. But what on earth could her teacher have told her parents? Her grades, despite her lack of effort, were always high, because her teacher valued one thing few people had in that school: critical sense. "Magdalena can think," she would say to her parents, in the parent-teacher conferences. She considered it now more of a flaw than a virtue, though. Those who did not think, like her classmates, seemed to live much better. She was a kind person, Mrs. Speranza, at least on the surface, and understanding. She even came across as sympathetic at times, but still she too was an adult, and as such an ally of her parents, not her own. Magdalena did not trust adults. And what did the teacher have to do with that doctor now? What were they talking about? She couldn't get the connection.

"You know well that once you start, there is no turning back," the voice added tersely.

"Yes, we know." This time her father's voice sounded strange, as if he was struggling to keep his emotions at bay. Her mother's sobs increased in intensity. Magdalena felt embarrassed for her. After all, her daughter was alive; what was there to yelp about like that? Why wasn't her father telling her to control herself? She wanted to get out of bed and yell at her to knock it off with all these scenes.

"We don't know what to do anymore. It's out of our control now," her father continued. "The doctors said we were very lucky this time, and we've heard that once before. I don't think there will be a third time. Heaven will not assist us anymore, I can feel it."

What an exaggeration. *Just give it a rest*, thought Magdalena. Her father seemed to her to be too melodramatic. And how her mother was sobbing. . . She would soon have a stroke if she kept this up..

Then there was a very long moment of silence. She thought Mom had been really overcome. Or maybe everyone had simply left. "All right," the doctor's voice was suddenly heard. "Let's try it."

Magdalena shivered and woke up suddenly. Now she was certain that she was not dreaming; she was actually in a shack. She felt completely drained of strength, but at least she had come to her senses. Perhaps she had really been in the hospital and reliving those moments had taken all her energy away. Her mother's sobs still rang in her ears. *Let's try it*, the doctor had said. What did he mean by that? She just didn't get it.

She looked at her hands and they were pale, but there were no needles or band-aids. She touched her face, her neck, her arms. She was sure she was awake. Unusual light and sounds were seeping in from the wooden boards on the walls; they sounded like dislodged leaves and birds. She sat up on the bed and had the unpleasant feeling of having a black hole instead of a stomach. Beside the stove, she noticed, was an ugly coffee table and a chair. And, on top of the coffee table, as out of place as the naked woman in that Manet painting, stood a plate with a cream-filled donut covered with chocolate frosting. It seemed to be watching her intently. She believed she was hallucinating; it was inviting and perfect, completely at odds with the squalor and abandonment of that place. For a moment, she even thought of eating a piece. Instead, as she often did when tempted like this, she turned away, toward the wall.

She tossed and turned in the hard, uncomfortable bed for what seemed like a very long time. She felt the evil and oppressive presence of food behind her.

"All right!" she suddenly shouted at the donut, sitting up on the bed. She grabbed it with one hand and devoured it in seconds, swallowing without even chewing. "Are you happy now?" she growled. Then, with residual strength from who knows where, she leapt off the bed, walked out of the shack and shoved two fingers down her throat, vomiting it all up.

She cried on the wooden steps in front of the door. She cried a lot, first, in silence, then — what did she care, with no one there anyway? — screaming like a little girl. It was a real release. She had wanted to cry like that for ages and who knows why she had never done it, she wondered now. She gasped, shaken by sobs she could no longer stop. But then she undoubtedly felt better. So much better that she burst out laughing. She needed to laugh like that, too, for no reason and with her throat wide open.

When that long moment of craziness ended, Magdalena stood as if intoxicated, looking at her feet and then around her. She was in a forest and it amazed her. There must have been a bunch of birds hiding in the branches, because they were making an incredible racket. It was surprisingly beautiful and soothing. Her vomit, there on the ground, clashed with all that cheerfulness. She stood up and walked around the hovel, following the pungent smell that had momentarily hit her nostrils.

There was a wooden building, long and narrow, with a ceiling so low that Magdalena hit her head when she tried to enter it. It was empty, but straw mixed with excrement was scattered on the floor. *Someone really should clean this up*, she thought, disgusted.

She went outside again and the sun, for a long moment, blinded her. She shielded herself with her hand until she got used to the light again. She did not want to be there. She slipped her hand into her pocket and noticed that the reassuring presence of her phone was missing.

She went back to the shack to look for it, but found nothing. The fire in the stove was dying out; a fetid bucket was abandoned in a corner. In general, a depressing squalor reigned in there. "I don't want to stay here," she thought again, this time aloud. "I have to escape."

She went outside as if possessed, looked around, and realized that she really had no idea where she was. All directions were equal. She ran to the right, in the direction of the sun, as if pursued by a horde of spirits. She ran as long as her lungs held out, zigzagging between the trees. She stopped and bent over to catch her breath; her vision blurred. She resumed walking, but felt her strength abandon her more and more. Her body, Magdalena knew, needed fuel. She thought of the donut turned into repulsive slime on the ground and almost regretted wasting it that way. She shook her head to push that thought down; she was certain that her will was stronger and more determined than her stomach and that, as always, she would be able to master it.

She walked by forcing her legs onward, dragging her feet on the ground and leaning against trees. She had to keep the sun in front of her at all times, she told herself, so she would not lose her way and waste energy she did not have. When she thought she recognized a tree she had already passed, she realized that she was losing her bearings. *Trees all look alike*, she thought. That one, however, had a strange trunk. She stopped to look at it: yes, it was the very same one she had noticed before, because it had a face, like in the Snow White movie, which she had watched with bated breath as a child. It seemed that the tree was staring at her in a way that revealed how little it was pleased with her. It appeared to be frowning, angry, and about to seize her with one of its branches.

For a moment, she felt a kind of fear, not of the tree, but of the idea of being stuck there, alone, for who knows how long. Whoever had brought her to that place had done so for a reason — even if she couldn't figure out what it was.

A hissing sound came from the mouth of the tree and made her gasp. For a moment, she thought she had heard it say her name. *The woods are shifty places*, she thought, *beautiful and threatening at the same time*. In the silence, the trees took on strange, almost human shapes and voices. She shrugged that silly idea off; she was 16 years old and had long since stopped believing such stories. To dispel her fears and prove to herself that there was no reason to be afraid, she stuck her hand in the hole of the tree. See, she reassured herself, there is nothing scary here.

But then something hairy moved in the hole, brushing against her hand, and Magdalena pulled back with a scream. The cry ricocheted off the trunks, and some birds hidden in the branches flew away in a flutter of wings. Magdalena instinctively ducked, protecting her head, imagining that the birds might fly at her and peck at her eyes. With her heart beating wildly, she told herself she had to leave this place as soon as possible.

She started walking again, but now she could think of nothing else but the thing that had brushed against her hand. What was it? She shuddered in disgust. She could not determine where the sun was now; she had lost clarity. The trees seemed to her to have grown taller, too tall, and the sky was distant, almost invisible. Looking upward she had a giddy feeling. Her body regained the upper hand over her will and Magdalena fell to the ground, unconscious.

She had a dream.

Perhaps it was a dream. Perhaps it wasn't.

It was certainly unusual; strange and yet very real. She was lying on the ground, she could feel this. She could smell and feel the dampness of the earth through her skin, under her fingers. She was sure that hours had passed since the escape began. An animal, perhaps a squirrel, approached her; Magdalena clearly felt its nose quiver very close to her cheek. She hoped it was not a mouse. Mice were repulsive to her. A feeling of dread was assailing her; she just wanted to run away before that beast could attract more of them and all at once start gnawing at her nose and fingers, but she was absolutely unable to move. Fortunately, then, the animal moved away from her face; Magdalena felt the vibrations of the ground caused by its hopping. Then followed a long time of nothingness.

The approach of stomping, confident, unhurried feet reawakened her senses. The footsteps stopped right beside her. Magdalena's foggy mind sensed that the owner of the feet was looking at her. All she could think was that he must find her extremely fat and disheveled. Then, unexpectedly, she felt herself lifted off the ground by a pair of firm, capable hands. How could he, whoever he was, manage to pick her up, heavy as she was?

It must have been almost night, since no light filtered through her closed eyelids. She did not open her eyes, because she could not; and it was a pleasant feeling, being carried like that, as if suspended in the air, but safely. The stranger holding her so firmly smelled good and exuded warmth. *He must be handsome, as well as strong*, she thought, as she persisted in not wanting to actually look. She knew anyway that there was not an ounce of energy in her body to invest in opening her eyes. She let herself be rocked for as long as it took. She almost slept, exhausted, as safe as she was in her mother's arms when she was a child. The stranger must have been very strong indeed to be able to walk all that time with her in his arms. She felt the warmth of his breathing on her face, which was beginning to become slightly labored. From the change in the sounds reaching her ears, she understood that she had arrived somewhere, indoors. She felt arms laying her on a bed. Only then, with an incredible effort of will, did she force her eyelids open.

It was dark. In the darkness she sensed only a silhouette. A white face, above her, staring at her without expression. She did not feel fear even for an instant. The man remained a few more moments beside the bed, his arms along his sides and his breath resuming a regular rhythm. Magdalena closed her eyes just long enough to blink, and when she opened them again, he was gone. If he had really been there, he was gone now, and without the slightest sound.

The next day, Magdalena woke up in a daze. For a moment, she was afraid that she had imagined everything: the run through the woods, the furry, invisible creature in the hole, the birds that wanted to peck at her eyes, and the fainting spell, as well as the guy who had brought her back by carrying her. When she had opened her eyes, in fact, it had felt like déjà-vu: she was on the bed, in the low-ceilinged wooden shed, and the chocolate-cream donut was back on the plate, staring at her. No matter how hard Magdalena tried, she could not put the facts in order and distinguish dream from reality. Instead, that was exactly what she needed. To convince herself that what had happened the day before really had happened, she walked out of the shed. Her vomit, now dry, was still there. She calmed down. Something real had happened, then.

She looked around for the mysterious man, although she was certain, without knowing why, that he would never show up again. The thought of him made her heart pound. She did not remember his smell, but she knew it was good. She had not seen him well, but she was sure he was beautiful. He was taking care of her, and it gave her some excitement. He would leave her food, and although he was not visible, he watched her from not too far away. She tasted the donut. The taste was good, undoubtedly, but it did not go down well with her. She stopped at the second bite, as soon as she felt nausea rise. Too sweet. Too big to finish.

The rest of the day was unending. Having nothing to do was as bad as it could get for her. In those moments of constrained pause there was a danger that her mind would begin to spin dangerously. Thoughts would come out of the dark corners to which she had relegated them and assail her from all sides. That's why she enjoyed loud music, the chaos of clubs, days spent talking about nothing with friends or flirting with boys. Anything to keep her mind off things. But what the heck could she do in that place where there was nothing? She walked around the shack, and her eye fell on the barn. A rake and a broom leaned against the frame of the little door. Okay, it wasn't the best idea, she told herself, but the alternative of being left alone with her thoughts was worse than setting out to shovel poop. Without giving it too much thought, she tied her hair in a tight knot on her head, lifted the hood of her sweatshirt, grabbed her tools, and went inside.

The small room was dark, but from the thin panes of light that stood out on the back wall, Magdalena guessed that there were small windows. She immediately went to open them to let in some fresh air. Then, patiently, and as if she had been doing it all her life, she began to push the dirty straw and manure to one side. She swept until packed earth appeared. Slowly, taking as much time as it took, she straightened out that abandoned place. Her mind, she marveled, thought of nothing, so the effort paid off. From time to time, she hummed some little tune from her childhood that randomly came to mind. Without feeling the repulsion she would have expected, she put the manure inside buckets she had found in a corner; then she took them out of the barn, emptying the contents into a single pile.

Who knows what her aristocratic "friends" from school or her fellow party-goers would have thought, seeing her prancing around piles of animal poop like that . . . They would have laughed at her, but the great discovery was finding out that she didn't care at that moment. They would think what they wanted. She hadn't felt like that in a long time. Relaxed and almost light.

When she re-entered the shack, she found a bucket of clean water. She felt excited at the thought that the stranger had once again been so close; it felt like she was playing some kind of exciting hide-and-seek game. She scrubbed her face and hands well. Dirt was smeared on her fingers. Despite her best efforts, she could not get the barn smell out of her hair and the dirt out from under her nails, from which the polish had peeled off almost completely. There was no mirror, but she did not need one to know that she looked awful. She left untouched on the table the plate of pasta she had found along with the water the stranger had brought her. She hadn't eaten pasta in years.

In the afternoon, she indulged in a walk and finished tidying up the barn. When she returned to the shack she found a surprise waiting for her: the pasta was gone, but over the embers of the stove an ear of corn had been placed to roast. Where they had found it, in that season, was a mystery. More importantly, how did the man know that she loved corn? The room was saturated with the good smell of it.

She sat down cross-legged in front of the stove and picked up the cob, scalding her fingers. Holding it with her sweatshirt, she brought it close to her face and filled her nostrils with its warm scent. She plucked the first kernel and savored it slowly, turning it over in her mouth. She crushed it with her tongue against her palate and the flavor exploded in her brain, bringing with it the memory of an entire summer of night swimming and barbecues. The last time she had eaten a corn cob had been with her parents, on the beach, under a starry sky. She remembered it vividly: she was 12 years old. She chased away the thought that had crept into her head, but she could not hold back the tear she had shed. One by one she consumed the kernels of the cob, eating it like this, slowly, until there were no more. Then she went to bed with a strange weight on her heart.

When Magdalena opened her eyes the next morning, she felt strangely good. A thought had made its way through the night, helped by the good taste of corn, and she had found it there when she woke up. She did not chase it away, because it was a happy thought. She had a feeling that a knot somewhere deep within her had been untied. She did not know who had brought her there and for what reason, but she knew for certain that it was a unique opportunity, one that someone had wanted to give her, and one that would not be repeated. It was exactly what she had been longing for, although she had not realized it until that morning. She wanted to get out of the drama that she had been living for too long and start a new script, with other outfits and sets and characters. She was tired of lying, of pretending to be someone else, of laughing even when things weren't funny at all, and of always having to raise the bar to get rid of boredom. Maybe she wouldn't be able to change, or maybe to do that she just had to take it one day at a time, like the kernels of corn she had eaten the night before, savoring them one by one.

She turned around, noticing a cheerful little fire that crackled in the stove. The mysterious man must have revived it for her, and the thought that he had been there while she slept still thrilled her. With the stove lit, the room already seemed less dreary. Magdalena had the absurd impression that the stove's mouth was smiling at her. She could not resist, and smiled back.

She had no desire to get up. It was a pleasant feeling to be warm, with her body relaxed and without having to do anything, without feeling the need to fill the silence. She tried hard to remember the man's face, but it appeared vague to her, like a dream. Her stomach grumbled with hunger. Even without looking, she knew that food had appeared on the table. She could smell it in the air. She allowed her eyes to verify: on a chipped plate, waiting to be eaten, peaceful and confident, was a huge sandwich stuffed generously with an inch of sliced meat. Magdalena sat down and only then, above her head, did she notice the paper.

EAT, PLEASE.

To one who had never felt what Magdalena felt about food, that order might have seemed simple; but not to her. Now, however, it was the mystery man telling her to eat. He wanted her to eat. Therefore, she would do it for him, for the stranger who cared for her.

She sat down at the table and took up the sandwich with circumspection, as if it were an unknown object that might explode at any moment. It would not fit in her hands, because of how long it was, and it certainly would not fit in her mouth. She looked at it from all sides, and it seemed to her that the sandwich was watching her. She began to nibble at it slowly, a little at a time, in small bites. The bread was fresh and crisped pleasantly between her fingers and under her teeth, sending out such an inviting smell that it filled her nostrils. Pleasure spread in successive waves throughout her body.

She ate with her eyes closed, savoring each bite with her mouth and nose, taking plenty of time. What was the hurry? She had nothing else to do and intended to make her benefactor happy with her. Besides, she had a certain amount of overdue hunger and was clutching the best sandwich in the universe between her fingers. I haven't *really* eaten in ages, she realized.

Having finished her meal, Magdalena sat for a moment longer, listening to her stomach. She had long since de-accustomed it to large quantities and had expected to feel it turn inside out, and then erupt all its contents. Instead, everything remained where it was, as if what she had needed up to that moment was precisely that boundless sandwich. Reassured, she got up and went outside. She breathed in the fresh, clean air, steeped in the woods, and thought that the air, too, could be good or bad. In her house, it always smelled stuffy and at school it had a smell all its own, indescribable, of too many people crammed together. The air on the street smelled of dirty clouds, wet iron, and manhole covers. But there, in the middle of nowhere, that had to be the original smell of the air. Even the pungent note coming from the barn did not clash with the rest.

She took a walk. She fervently hoped that the mysterious man would find something for her to do or, better yet, let her see him. It would have been nice to live there, just the two of them. It was reassuring to know that there was someone who cared for her. Then her mind, by contrast, raced to the world outside of there. This time Magdalena did not try to stop it.

She reviewed the faces of those she hung out with and felt her heart become sad and overwhelmed. She had never had anything in common with her classmates, and it could not have been otherwise. She had not befriended anyone in class; she always felt judged by them and in turn mercilessly judged them as poor half-wits. They only thought about studying and planning their future lives and did not know how to have fun. Then there was Eliza, with whom she shared shopping and the thrills of clubbing. But, without these pastimes, nothing remained between them. And then, there were Luke, Rex, Jack — her stomach tightened. They were always nice, but probably only because they wanted that one thing from her. . . At that thought, which she had brooded about within herself for years without ever really giving it space, Magdalena collapsed to the ground in tears. She had lied to her parents many times, and also to herself. She had thrown herself away by silencing that part of her that tried to rebel, to say that happiness was something else. When had all that crap started?

She cried for a long time, unable to stop. She thought of the times she had ended up in the hospital and of her parents' terrified faces, and of that video they had filmed without her knowledge one time when she got high, just for laughs. She didn't even recognize herself, and she had been frightened, watching herself reduced like that. Yet she had laughed, to hide that the sight of that other Magdalena, whom she neither remembered nor knew, horrified her. The tears did not stop coming, along with the bad memories, the experiences that had led her to be what she was now. She groaned inside. She wanted to love herself, she wanted to treat herself well, because the life she had chosen for the past two years, she now realized, had almost killed her.

Only when evening began to fall did she feel as if she had run out of tears. She felt exhausted and her face was swollen. She went back into the shack to wash up.

She gasped: on the table, in the corner, was a plate of pot roast and a blue notebook with a pen. Magdalena ran to the door; she wanted to see the stranger at any cost.

There was no one there.

"Hey! Where are you?" she shouted, taking courage, her voice hoarse from crying so much.

She was answered only by a group of birds that were startled from the nearest trees. She returned and sat down at the table. She read the sign again.

EAT, PLEASE.

She had never been particularly fond of meat, and she had already made an exception for sliced meat in that sandwich. With the tip of her fork she touched a slice. It looked very soft, and without her being able to control it, saliva collected in her mouth. She smiled at her reaction and put the fork down.

In a moment, she told herself. She had one more thing to do first.

She opened the notebook and stared at the gleaming white pages. She ran her arm over her puffy eyes and eyelashes sticky with tears. She clicked the pen tip out and began.

> I know when it all started. I know the first step I took, the first real lie that brought me here. I have only myself to blame, though. Only myself. I can't blame it on anyone else.
>
> I was 13 years old and I was doing everything I could to prove myself. Marco was my rhythmic

gymnastics coach. He was 25 years old. It seemed unbelievable to me that a big, handsome guy like him would be interested in me, of all people. My teammates would have given anything to be in my place. Instead, he wanted me. He had told me, "I want you, Magdalena." That's right. "I want you," looking into my eyes in a way that left no escape.

Magdalena shuddered at the memory of that evening when he, at the end of training, had waited for her at the door when the others had already left and, with hot breath on her neck, had whispered those words in her ear. Then he had looked at her in that piercing way of his, waiting for an answer that, in fact, she could see he was already certain of. She had swallowed, in astonishment, and nodded her head. Then he had smiled, gorgeous. Magdalena would have given anything to forget that moment, which remained sharp before her eyes even now, and which she had retraced like a nightmare for months and months after it had happened. Along with everything else. Her shaking hand tightened around the pen.

He had arranged everything; I just had to tell a lie to my parents. Without thinking about it too much, I did. I said I was going to sleep over at a gymnastics partner's house, and she backed me up. After practice, however, I wandered around by myself for a while. I felt big and free. I even went into a coffee shop and, without really knowing why, I ordered a coffee. Me, who hates coffee, by the way. The barista eyed me from top to bottom ("You're more of a chocolate milk kind of gal," his face said) and I still have imprinted in my mind my dirty pink purse, with a few crumbs in it and

Hello Kitty's face on it. With a pounding heart, I
finally took the bus and after 20 minutes got off
in front of the hotel he had told me about. When
I think about how excited I was – what an idiot! I
knew perfectly well what he wanted from me and
I thought I wanted it too.

But, when we were alone in the room, I felt that
something was wrong. Everything was perfect, it
seemed, but something inside me was not right. By
then it was too late to change my mind. Besides, he
was really handsome and I was so convinced that
I loved him. And that he loved me. I was afraid, so
afraid, and together we couldn't wait.

As those distant moments surfaced, large drops fell
on the notebook, rippling the paper. Thinking back now,
in that room, with her school bag still on her shoulders,
Magdalena saw herself as small, very small indeed.
Years later, she felt pity for that little girl, as if she were
not even her, but a younger sister. Her heart clenched
and she wished she had a time machine to go back and
yell at her to run away, because everything that had
come after had started right there.

She squinted her eyes to get a better look; through
the tears it was as if the sentences were rolling out of
the pen, unable now to stop. No one would read those
lines anyway, so she could say anything, even what she
had never had the courage to talk about, even with her
closest friends.

Instead, it was just ugly and bleak. At the end of it
all, I felt strange and excited. I asked him if the two
of us, at that point, were together. I was convinced
we were, but I wanted to hear it from his mouth.
Instead, he stared at me with disdain. His words

*are burned into my heart in block letters. Capital
letters. "DO YOU REALLY THINK I COULD LIKE A
FAT GIRL LIKE YOU?"*

She re-lived this as she wrote, with the same intensity as then, the twinge of pain that had hit her when
Marco had thrown these cruel words in her face. And
then, indelible in her memory, was Marco's toughened
face, that seemed to take pleasure in hurting her that
way.

> *I kept quiet and cried while he put his clothes back
> on. He walked out, leaving me there alone, without
> even looking back. He had gotten what he wanted.
> It was the worst night of my life; I was so afraid,
> alone in that ugly place, full of ugly noises. I was
> terrified that someone would come and knock on
> the door of the room and discover me still there.
> Or worse, that he would throw me out, in the
> middle of the street, in that suburban neighbor-
> hood near the highway. I didn't know what to do. I
> had never been in that area before. I wanted to call
> Mom and Dad, but how could I explain why I was
> there? I felt all dirty. Old. Already rejected. I had
> become Little Red Riding Hood. I had never really
> understood that story, until I became the main
> character. The hunter never came, though. There
> is no hunter in the real story of Little Red Riding
> Hood. She just gets eaten, and it serves her right.*

She still felt furious with herself because she had been
so stupid to fall for this trick. To believe that someone
would find her beautiful and love her the way she was.
That's what happened to trust. And after that, it was too

late to go back. Some things are lost forever, never to be recovered, and you have to move on with what's left.

> *At practice, then, I tried to avoid him in every way. I couldn't even make eye contact with him. My partner must have told the others that I had been with him, because they started asking me questions. I would answer with an air of superiority that, yes, I mean, it hadn't been that great. And they laughed and didn't believe it, and one night Marco even took me to one side in the locker room, after they had all left, and slapped me. For a moment everything went black. He threatened me: I had to stop telling people that he hadn't been great, or he would tell everyone I was a slut. And he was going to tell my parents. That's when I got scared. Thinking about it now, it's clear that he would never have done that, because then he would have gotten in trouble. But I didn't know that at the time; I didn't even think about it. It seemed possible and I believed him. What would my parents have said if they had known? That thought didn't give me a wink of sleep. I was convinced they would have thrown me out of the house. Yes, on reflection now even that was a stupid idea, and yet I was really sure that it would happen. Maybe, if I had spoken up right away, they would have defended me and it would have been Marco who would have gotten in trouble. Certainly, everything that came later would not have come to pass.*

For the first time, Magdalena realized that not eating was a way for her to get her parents' attention. It was like shouting, "Help!" but without being too noticeable. In fact, when her parents got angry at the table because she wouldn't touch food, the bad part of her would awaken and make her jump to her feet, screaming like a demon. She didn't know why she did that, either. She wanted to be helped, but she did not want to be helped. She wanted her parents to see that something was wrong, but she was afraid that the truth would come out and that they would find out what she had done. She resumed writing.

> *I stopped going to the gym by telling myself that I got tired of gymnastics, even though I loved it. And then . . . I stopped eating. Until he had said those cruel words to me, I had never thought of myself as fat. After that day, though, I couldn't help seeing myself as chubby every time I looked in the mirror. But even trying hard, even if I went without eating for a month, I quickly realized that my body could not change, because I have massive bones like those of a wooly mammoth. Even if I lost the last layer of fat, they remain what they are.*
>
> *"You have a pretty face," everyone tells me, and it's true. I like my face and the boys like it too. Actually, they like the rest of me as well.*
>
> *However, even though I have a ton of guys following me, I always feel like Marco is watching me. And even though I don't give a damn about him and what he thinks anymore, what he said always comes back to me and feels true. I want to erase it, I want to not give it so much weight, but I can't. I eat and I feel guilty. Then I throw up. Then I feel even more guilty. I hate my body and I starve it, I punish it. I hate myself because I am weak.*

At that moment, the scent of meat made her nostrils quiver. She stared at the plate and then at the notebook.

That's how it all started. I was young, naive, and he took advantage of me. It happens. Serves me right.

Magdalena put down her pen. She felt better; writing had helped her gain clarity. She had kept everything inside for so long, and those ugly truths had consumed her, like a parasite feeding on her anxieties. Now she had pulled them out of herself and thrown them, black on white, into the notebook. They had come out of her; they no longer possessed her.

She took the plate and sat down on the doorstep, resting it on her lap. She took the first bite and the fat melted in her mouth like butter. She had never tasted such good meat. She usually threw the fat away. She ate the whole thing and wished for more braised meat. It was as if her body was demanding the food she had denied it for too long.

She did not know where she was or how she had ended up there, much less why. Yet she did not want to be anywhere else.

She slept soundly through the night. For the first time in a long time, she felt at peace with the world and with herself. She did not hear the light footsteps that entered the shack, the faint sound of the empty dish being withdrawn and replaced with a full one. Nor did she perceive the gaze of the man who stood beside her bed for a few moments, watching her seriously and thoughtfully. But even in her sleep Magdalena knew that she was not alone; that there was someone nearby, taking care of her, and that was enough for her. She was tired. All her past was still pressing on her shoulders, and until she got rid of the weight of it, she would not be able to breathe the fresh air of that place deeply.

Then there was Andrew. Frederick, of course, the senior. And Constantine, the jealous one. I could never break up with him; it scared me when he got angry. Fortunately, then I got involved with Nicholas, who set him straight on a few things. He was stronger than Constantine and fought for me. For a while, I even believed he cared about me, but then he met that other one – the skinny one. After that I was with. . . what was the name of the Albanian guy, with a crocodile tattoo on his arm? It's crazy, but I can't remember his name anymore. We were together for a few weeks, certainly less than a month. I can't remember everyone's name; they would come and go and they usually dumped me for one reason or another. Why was I acting that way? I felt like I had made a mistake and the mistake was not fixable. I had fallen and could not get up. It was impossible to go back to before that night when I was in that dingy room with Marco. Everyone said that love is beautiful, and a part of me felt it had to be. I wished with all my being that it was but, in fact, it never was. Each time, I found that the guy of the moment didn't really care about me. I would give him everything, really everything, because I wanted him to love me. But after a few intense months, it would end.

Then I met Eliza. She said she had a lot of fun teasing the boys. That it was she who decided who she went with, and who didn't make the cut. And then, after using them, she would drop them. Well, I don't know if she was sincere. Maybe something bad had happened to her and like me she was ashamed to talk about it, or maybe she really liked living that way. I tried to do as she did, too, but in the end, when I reflect on it now, I can't tell who was using whom. Once, someone even tried to give me money. How shameful, thinking about it now!

*Anyway, in the end, one lie led to another, and I
didn't even know how to get out of it anymore, or
what the truth was. I used to tell myself that it was
okay, that I was all grown up now; that the world
is lousy and people are lousy; that the stories they
tell you in books or movies don't exist. Real love
doesn't exist; it's just a word to mask the desire for
something else. I certainly am not capable of love.
And no one has ever really loved me.*

This last sentence turned her stomach. She felt that
writing was good for her, undoubtedly, but at the same
time it caused her intense pain. It was as if nails were
digging into her chest. Yet she had to get it all out. She
was sure the stranger knew it, too; that was why he
had left her the notebook and all those hours of solitude, to stay with herself to reflect and cleanse. It was
necessary to make room for something beautiful, like
a room crammed with old and useless stuff that needs
to be cleared out so that light and newness can enter.
She sensed that the stranger had something unique in
mind for her, which might even make her feel happy for
the first time in a long time. The mysterious promise of
some serenity she felt mounting inside kept her going
day by day in a hut in the middle of the woods.

Magdalena got out of bed. She had written late into
the night, lit by the iridescent flames of the stove. After-
ward, she had slept soundly. Her hand had ached from
all the writing, but each memory brought out another,
like a jar full of demons that once opened could not be
closed. Even the episodes she had forgotten, and those
that had been buried by alcohol or pills, had resurfaced,
frightening and disheartening. Everything, everything

she had thrown up. It had hurt her, like a medicine that purges the body of illness; painful but necessary. She had cried a lot, berated herself, and finally...

I am a fool. I hurt myself a lot. I was as if launched down an increasingly steep slope and couldn't brake. Then someone caught me on the fly before I smashed myself to pieces. He is my mystery man. He did it, with the help of my parents and I still haven't figured out who else. This situation is totally absurd. I have been alone for days in a wooden shack in the middle of a forest. I don't talk to anyone, I haven't washed for too long, and I smell like crap. And then, I eat again. I have started to love myself a little. And it's not true that no one has ever loved me. My parents love me. Maybe even the mystery man who takes care of me loves me. No guy has ever been able to care for me the way he does; no one has been able to read me so well inside. He knows what I need even before I figure it out. Until today, I haven't gotten one thing right and I've always tried to be loved by the wrong people. I understand now, though. I also understand that what has been cannot be erased, but that it is always possible to start from scratch. I cannot forget the past but I can move forward. First of all by forgiving myself.

Marco, no, I cannot forgive him. In fact, when I get out of here I might go to the police. Yes, maybe I will go there. And maybe I'll even go after him, because I want him to know what he did to me. But I don't know if I will have the courage to look him in the eye and really talk to him. Just remembering his face makes me sick to my stomach.

Instead, I forgive that 13-year-old girl who took the bus to meet her great love. I forgive her, because she could not have known that she would get burned.

It was not her fault.

It was not my fault.

Magdalena had lost track of the days. In fact, she had never kept track of them, because she was in no hurry to leave, to return to her usual life. She reread the last lines she had written the night before. She almost couldn't remember them anymore, as if they had come out of the pen without her noticing, or someone who was not her had written them. But yes, it was true, she forgave herself.

Magdalena forgave Magdalena.

She picked up the notebook, whose pages, wetted with tears, had become all wavy and had grown in volume. She giggled; for a moment it seemed funny to her. Then, crouching in front of the stove, she brought the diary closer to the flames for them to eat it. She watched the fire lap at the blue cover, as if to taste it; then, more convinced, it began to devour everything, coming close enough to scorch her fingertips.

"Here," Magdalena said, speaking to the flames as if they were a living thing, finally tossing what remained of the notebook into the stove's mouth.

The pages were consumed in moments. The ashes were piled at the bottom, and Magdalena scattered them with a twig. They fluttered in a swirl of gray shreds, before turning to dust. Only then did Magdalena look up and notice that the writing on the sign had changed.

WELL DONE.
READ, PLEASE.

With a quick glance she walked across the room. What was she supposed to read? Around there, excluding the sign, there was absolutely nothing to read. Maybe it was a joke – or maybe a metaphor. Was she supposed to read inside herself? Apart from the fact that Magdalena had done nothing else for the past few days, so far the stranger had always been clear in his demands. Eat and write, although the latter had been more of a suggestion that she had freely taken.

She opened the door of the shack and, at her feet, like an abandoned child before a church door, was a book. She picked it up: *The Adventures of Pinocchio*. Now this had to be a joke. A children's book? She was hurt: who did he take her for? At school, they made her read certain pieces of ancient and modern literature, even in foreign languages. Stupid educational children's stories had no appeal to her. She had never read *Pinocchio*; it had been enough for her to see the cartoon when she was three years old to lose all interest. She re-entered the house and threw the book on the bed. She felt a kind of distaste for that story; the few things she knew about it bothered her, even physically.

She went out into the fresh air to stretch her legs, to shake off the exaggerated discomfort that stupid book had given her. It wounded her to think that the mysterious man, more than a woman, thought of her as a child. She walked away from the shack and the book, muttering to herself and kicking at the piles of rotten leaves and stones she encountered as she walked. Still, was it possible that the man who, up to that point, had shown he knew her so well, who had changed her heart with a kernel of corn, had been wrong? What had he wanted to say to her, giving her that book to read? If she had done so, surely he would have liked for her to read it. And Magdalena wanted him to like her at all costs. If only for that reason, she told herself at last, I will read it.

She was back after a good hour. The forest air had put a certain appetite in her. When she returned to the cabin, the book was no longer on the bed. It was on top of the coffee table, gracefully lying next to a cup of hot chocolate.

"Okay, I get it," Magdalene said aloud, amused and flattered by the stranger's insistence.

She trusted him and wanted to make him happy, although this time her request seemed unnecessary and meaningless. She sat down at the table and dipped a finger in the chocolate. She sucked it lazily, lost in thought. Then, slowly, as if it was ritualistic, she drank the rest, enjoying it with her eyes closed and letting the steam condense on the tip of her nose. The book was already open to the first page and seemed to look at her expectantly. Finally, she gave in: with her mittens on the table and her face in her hands, she blew away the hair that fell back on her face and began to read.

ELIJAH

When he opened his eyes, he was in a forest. The throbbing bump on his head screamed to him that it had not been a dream.

He was at the usual club. Everyone was looking for him; word had gotten out that he had the best stuff, so he hadn't been surprised to find himself confronted by a 30-year-old mommy's boy. With a quick glance he had scrutinized the expensive watch on his wrist and the goofy face. He looked harmless, and he could certainly pay.

"Do you want me to stay with you?" Rocco had asked him.

Elijah had gauged the guy with another look, confirming his first impression: harmless imbecile. And anyway, if needed, he could defend himself and counterattack. He was bigger and taller than the puny fellow.

"Go ahead," he had said to Rocco, feeling invulnerable. "What do you need?" he had then asked the customer harshly. This man was twice his age, but he was the one who had the stuff, so he had the power.

"Are you Elijah?" the guy had asked him.

From something in his voice, Elijah smelled a cop. He had made to leave, but another guy, over six feet tall and seeming just as wide, had appeared behind him out of nowhere, closing off his escape route. At that, Elijah had thrown himself at the thinner guy, but the guy had moved with the agility of a boxer and he had ended up on the floor, hitting his head on a garbage can. What an idiot he had been, sending Rocco away and exposing himself like that! He had overestimated himself and, more importantly, underestimated the guy. Or rather, the guy had deliberately been playing the idiot. He had stood motionless and stared at him without expression. Elijah had seen him give an almost imperceptible nod to his companion, who had approached slowly, also expressionless as an iceberg. Then he had leaned down and extended a steely hand to hold him still. Elijah had wriggled like an eel, and he had guessed from the guy's expression that he was giving him a hard time. Perhaps he had not expected to find Elijah so strong. *I can bite him*, he had thought, but the gorilla had anticipated his move and, with unexpected speed for one of his size, he had raised his elbow and struck, aiming straight for the carotid artery.

That was the last image his memory had retained. He rubbed his neck; it hurt at the spot where that brick house of a man had hit him. Finally, Elijah looked around, still dazed, but already feeling anger swelling inside him like an avalanche. He was lying on the ground in a forest, that much was evident. And for quite a while, too, judging by the moisture his clothes had absorbed. The question was, where am I? To his recollection, he knew of no forests in his neighborhood. There was a lake, yes, and a bunch of shopping malls, but woods, no. Why had they dumped him here? Elijah racked his brain, trying to guess who he had to thank for this unpleasant awakening. He had several enemies, a bunch of people envious of him, but this was a decidedly ridiculous method of getting him off the streets.

Wherever he was, however, he was going to make it home. He was just annoyed that he had to struggle, walk maybe for hours. He got to his feet, shaking the leaves off his clothes. Once he got out of there, he would find out who had played this little trick on him and make them pay. He had his friends, too. He looked for his cell phone in his pocket. He could always call his father or Rocco; someone would come for him.

When he discovered that he had nothing left on him, he felt naked. The phone, the money, the pills — all gone, stolen. He had been knocked out and robbed like a moron. He was blinded by anger.

"Show yourself, asshole!" he shouted to the woods, but his voice was lost in the open space.

There was no response. Only a bird, startled, took flight from a branch. Elijah looked up at the brightening sky. This was the time he usually headed back home, so his father must not be alarmed yet. By now, his father knew he would not return until the morning, about 10 hours later than the curfew that was imposed on him.

His father. What a schmuck. A Protestant pastor in a world where people no longer believed in anything. Or at most their stomachs, Elijah told himself as he heard his own's fierce growling. At home, they were starving. His brother was perfect; he had graduated with honors from high school and was already working to contribute to the family's expenses. All the while, Elijah was flunking out and had to repeat senior year for the third time. School had never mattered to him. "Your brother was so good. . ." the teachers would tell him. But I'm not him, you fools! Haven't you noticed? He would look at them cockily from under his hat, going about his own business. Yeah, he wasn't his brother. Fortunately. He,

Elijah, earned money too, and quite a bit of it, but by the methods *he* chose and certainly not to give any to his parents. He had bought a ring for his girlfriend and a brand of shoes that no one had yet. And he collected hats, in every color, some for every day and some for important occasions, like the shiny one he wore when he went around with Martina. Martina — he had not sent her the usual good-night message, so certainly she, at least, had been alarmed. He had never failed to text her before bed for almost a year. But even so, what could Martina have done? Elijah's parents were black. *They hate her*, he thought, *because she is a pretty blond who talks like a longshoreman and doesn't mind that I am a slacker.* Martina liked him even more because of this, he bet: good girls in high school liked to be with bad boys in vocational school. And, as far as he was concerned, he had a thing for blondes.

The sun was rising. He brushed the leaves out of his frizzy hair and looked around for his hat; without it he looked like just any other guy, but with the visor down he could have set the world on fire. Yes, that was something to think about, setting the damned woods on fire to see if anyone came to put it out. He looked for his lighter in his pants pocket, but he already knew he wouldn't find it; they had patted him down pretty good. And there was no sign of the hat either.

He kept his anger in check only because he wanted to keep his wits about him and think his way out of this place. He searched the surroundings with watchful eyes, and something at the foot of a fairly distant tree caught his eye. It was a piece of paper folded in quarters. Elijah hoped he would finally find out who had brought him there, but was stunned when he opened the paper and found that it was some kind of map. What was this, a treasure hunt?! In a fit of rage, he crumpled up the map. Was he being toyed with? But then he weighed the alternatives: either he refused to go along with the prank, doing his own thing and wandering haphazardly around the place, or he followed the map. He dug out of his memory the clock's method of finding north. He had learned it as a child, when they had tried to send him to scouts, and he was surprised that he still remembered it. He hoped he had not made a mistake when he lined up the map and walked south, in the direction of the spot marked with an X. He did not know where he was or where he was going, but it certainly made more sense than standing there.

He hated walking, having no alternative but to obey a map. The smell of the woods disgusted him, like the mud and leaves that stuck to his shoes and the bush branches that grasped his clothes and scratched his hands. *If I had a machete or a flamethrower, I would raze this place to the ground,* he thought; *the woods have no reason to exist.*

It took him at least two hours to reach the spot, and he was not at all surprised to find a dilapidated shack. What had he expected, a hotel? Or a surprise party? The door was open. Inside, with a quick glance, he saw a bed that looked soggy and a cast-iron stove, a bucket, and a slingshot. It smelled of mold and piss. He took a walk around the inside of the shack and rummaged through every nook and cranny; there was absolutely nothing to eat, and he was bloody hungry. The realization made him furious. He kicked the bed and the wooden leg broke off, causing it to collapse on its side with the mattress. Then he grabbed the stove pipe and with a howl of rage ripped it off the wall where it was nailed. With the pipe he struck blindly at the walls, the bed, and the stove. With his kicks, he reduced the bucket to an unrecognizable scrap of iron. When there was nothing left to destroy, he came out of the shed again. He was breathing hard and felt possessed by a murderous rage. He noticed a bird flying away from the canopy of a tree. If there is a bird, he reasoned, there is also its nest. He climbed nimbly and found it. He stole all the eggs and cracked them directly into his mouth, one after another. They were small and tasteless. Then an idea came to him; he climbed again, this time reaching the top of the tree. He rotated his gaze all around, three hundred and sixty degrees. Far away, to the north, there was smoke. Good, it meant he was not alone. He didn't think twice — he got out of the tree and walked on.

He had been plodding on for several minutes when the sky suddenly darkened at an inconceivable speed. Lightning flashed across it, blinding Elijah; it must have struck very close. The air was electric. Just as he decided to turn on his heels and run back toward the hut, a torrential downpour crashed upon his head. He threw himself, now soaked, inside the shack, while the storm raged on. Thunder rattled the walls, and lightning flashed brightly through the forest, over which night seemed to fall before it should. Elijah took off all his clothes and pulled the mattress off the lopsided bed. He threw himself on it, wrapping himself haphazardly in the only blanket he found. It was rough and it smelled, but he had slept in far worse places. He fell asleep to the rhythmic tapping of the rain on the tin roof, laughing at the faces of those who had dumped him there thinking they were doing him in.

The cold woke him. He had no idea how long he had slept. It was daylight outside. He gasped as he noticed a sign hanging on the wall behind him.

CUT DOWN THE MARKED TREES,
PLEASE.

The idea that he had been fooled again, and that the bastard on the map had been just a stone's throw away from him without his hearing, made him instantly outraged. What did he want now? He had to cut down what?! In disbelief he walked out of the hut and saw that some of the trees in the woods had been marked with an X in red paint. Not far away, on the ground, he noticed what would be his tool: an old saw too small and rusty to do anything. The purpose, he guessed on the fly, was surely to keep him busy for a long time. And whoever was behind it had been smart enough to avoid providing him with a hatchet. *Who knows what I could have done with it,* he thought with his vision clouded by uncontrollable fury. He bit his lips until they were bloody. Then he climbed back to the top of the tallest tree, discovering that the smoke was still there.

He trudged through a bog that reached to his ankles. His new shoes would have to be thrown away, and it infuriated him. His wet clothes, which he had no choice but to put back on, were freezing cold. He tried to come up with an idea, since hunger was making him even more livid. He spotted another inhabited nest and snapped the neck of the brooding mother, just for the heck of it. He drank the usual eggs, always too small and useless. Whoever put me here will pay dearly, he kept telling himself. It was clear that the guy he had met at the club, together with the troll, was not a policeman; the police cage you, they don't abandon people in the woods. But the whole thing must have been much more complicated than that; it was all too well organized. He suspected that his father had a hand in it. He must have been so desperate by now to try this last ridiculous move to save him! A rickety laugh escaped his throat and echoed sinisterly in the woods; too bad he had no intention of being saved.

Life was like that — the law of the jungle ruled. Those who were too weak and had no balls would succumb to it. He felt strong and smart, able to survive even in this place, if only by feeding on his anger. Someone like his father could never understand, and in fact he must have believed that dumping him in the middle of a forest cutting trees with a blunt saw would change his ways.

He marched for hours without feeling the slightest fatigue. In the afternoon, he reached a shack similar to the one he had left. Behind it was someone whistling. Elijah took a walk around.

There was a large field, surrounded by piles of stones, furrowed by neat rows of cabbages. In the middle stood a boy in blue overalls sloshing buckets of water over the plants. He stood watching him, unseen, for a while. When the buckets were empty, the guy picked them up and walked away from the fenced area.

Then Elijah entered the shed. There was no food there either, he discovered with disappointment. There was a hat, though. It was filthy and smeared with sweat, but still he absolutely needed it. He shoved it on his head, lowering the visor over his eyes. Already he felt better.

Then he went out and sat down on a pile of rocks, waiting for the guy to show up again.

It was taking so long – where on earth was he going to get water, the Pacific? Elijah saw him reappear with his forearms swollen from exertion, his face red, and his shoulders hunched. A lot of water must have spilled on the way back. *A futile effort*, Elijah thought; *who was making him do it?*

When Daniel looked up, he almost dropped his buckets in surprise. He was no longer used to seeing people, and he certainly did not expect it at that moment. The first thing he thought was that finally the guy leaving him food and signs had shown up. Black? He had imagined him looking very different. Then he got a better look at him; he was a guy just like him. And he had swiped his hat. All the tranquility gained through solitude and work was erased by the anger provoked upon seeing something of his own on someone else's head.

"Hey," he said without preamble, striding aggressively toward the stranger. "Give me back my hat."

The other challenged him directly. "Come and get it," he said with a grin, rising to his feet.

Daniel measured his opponent with a quick glance before attacking; the intruder was much taller than he was. He wasn't necessarily stronger, though, he told himself, and his bravado might just be enough to intimidate the other. Daniel felt confident; all the slogging of those weeks had toughened him up, and he had already been good at fighting before.

The guy looked at him as if to say, " What? Are you afraid?" and he adjusted the hat on his head to reiterate the notion that he now owned it. At that point, Daniel accepted the provocation and rushed toward him. He started with a shove and with satisfaction saw his opponent stagger. It was evident from his face that he had not expected to encounter that much force, but he recovered quickly from his surprise and responded by pushing him back. Daniel, on the other hand, had anticipated this and grabbed onto his jacket, using his own strength against him. He stuck his leg between his to throw him off balance, but they both fell to the ground. They rolled, trying futilely to overpower each other. They struggled for a while, at first testing each other, then letting their instincts take over. To pain they responded with more pain. The first real punch made Daniel's jaw creak, and he responded with a headbutt right in his opponent's face. Elijah stood dazed for a moment, but he regained his focus. When he saw a trickle of blood coming out of his opponent's nose, Daniel's courage swelled. For a moment, the absurd idea had crossed his mind that he was invulnerable. But it was only with an enormous effort that he managed to get back on his feet. The guy wiped away the blood with his sleeve and approached menacingly. Daniel did not miss the sinister light in his eyes and felt a chill run down his spine. He did not move an inch, but for a moment he was certain that the guy could beat him to a pulp.

The two boys looked at each other like ferocious animals, waiting to spot their opponent's weak point to attack. Elijah snapped a few times to see if the other would be intimidated. Daniel sustained his gaze and dodged the false attacks by standing up to him. All around, the forest seemed to have become deserted; only the wheezing, gasp-like breaths of the two boys could be heard. Tired of the game, eventually Elijah stretched out his arm to grab Daniel with a lightning gesture which he was not quick enough to dodge. They were fighting hand-to-hand again, feeling each other's hot breath on their faces. Elijah tightened his hand around Daniel's neck, and Daniel immediately did the same. They began to clench angrily, staring into each other's eyes, determined not to let go, even to the point of not being able to do it anymore, or to see the other collapse breathlessly. Daniel's vision blurred, but when he noticed a shadow of a smile on Elijah's face, he summoned what little strength he had left and squeezed with all the hatred in his body. Elijah's victorious expression changed abruptly; he felt the air in his lungs running out, and no more was passing from his throat. Suddenly it was clear, and they read it in each other's faces, that they would both win, or both lose. They were deadlocked in a perfect balance. A glance was enough to share that thought and plant it simultaneously. They released their grip by pushing each other back to separate, putting as much space as possible between them. Depleted of strength, they threw themselves to the ground catching their breath. Then, after a long time, Daniel first extended a hand in a sign of truce.

"Daniel."

He tried to keep his voice steady, though he struggled to get it out of his sore throat.

"Elijah."

He squeezed it out.

Each immediately recognized himself in the other, and saw that they could even become friends someday.

"Now give me my hat back," Daniel said with a forced smile.

"No way," replied Elijah with another smile, but not at all friendly.

That was not comrade behavior; there was a code to be followed. Still, Daniel had been moving tons of water all morning, leaking blood from various parts, and feeling his face and body pummeled. He didn't have the strength to fight back at that moment. He decided he would wait for a better opportunity to take back what was his (actually, he too had swiped that cap, on the first day of school, from a 14-year-old in his class. Not the same boy as the watch, though).

"If you help me make four more trips, then I'll buy you dinner," Daniel proposed, trying to strike a deal. The unforeseen combat had consumed all his strength and he was certain he would not be able to get the job done alone.

"You have food?!" Elijah squinted; in the shed earlier he had found nothing.

"No, not really," Daniel explained. "To get food, you have to work: those who don't work, don't eat."

Elijah burst into explosive laughter, which greatly vexed Daniel.

"What's so funny?"

"You sound like my old man. He always says those exact words. What, are you, a minister too?"

"I hate priests," Daniel cynically made his position clear at once. In fact, his uncle, a priest who was in Romania, was one of the kindest people he had ever met. But certainly all other ministers and priests sucked.

"So that makes two of us. My old man is like a priest. Evangelical, though. But they're all of the same breed anyway."

"Yeah," Daniel wanted to end the conversation.

He glanced quickly upward; the sky was darkening and he was sure that if he did not get the job done, the quantity of dinner food would decline.

"Well? Are you going to help me or not?" He pointed Elijah toward the empty buckets.

"Not a chance," he laughed in response.

"Suit yourself."

Daniel turned away. He thought it was clear that Elijah had never experienced the hunger he had in those early days in the woods. And that he did not know the rules of the situation.

"Go on, slave," mocked Elijah, laughing at him boisterously.

Daniel, trying his best to control himself, ignored him and went back and forth eight more times, head down and mute as an ox, letting nothing betray his weariness. He wanted to show the black guy what he was made of. In fact, although he was doing much better than in the first weeks, his arms were in pieces.

When he finished with the last bucket, Elijah gave him a round of applause that was the epitome of his mockery. "Good little puppet!"

Laugh, laugh, Daniel thought, grinding his teeth, *but I'm eating and you're not.*

Now the best part of the day began for him. In the morning, when he opened his eyes, he was rested but aware of all the toil that awaited him outside the door for the rest of the day. By sunset, he was so tired that he could hardly change his clothes, but he had such a sense of peace about him that could not be explained. The stove, the food, Kitty: they seemed like nothing, but they had become everything.

He ignored Elijah and went to the shack. The food was in its usual place, and seeing it was refreshing. He always feared he had not been good enough; it had happened more than once that dinner was meager because he had not tried hard enough.

"You eat!" he heard Elijah's voice behind him.

"Don't even think about it," he warned him darkly.

But the other guy didn't even hear him; he violently shrugged him off by sending him crashing against the wall, grabbed the can of broccoli, opened it and gobbled up the contents in twenty seconds flat, slurping it all up and swallowing without chewing.

"Hey!" protested Daniel, who by now was seeing red.

"What do you want?" quipped the other with his mouth full. "I haven't eaten in a day! And this stuff makes you puke, too."

"But I've been working," Daniel replied curtly.

"Good dummy!" Elijah grabbed the bread, biting into it. "You work and I eat," he commented, chewing, spitting bread crumbs and taunts in Daniel's face.

Daniel was so inflated with rage that he no longer even felt fatigue. Rendered blind and reckless by wrath, just as Elijah had done two days earlier with the troll and the puny man, he charged, snorting like a bull. Elijah ducked and he ended up slamming his face against the stove. He fell to the floor, unconscious.

When Daniel opened his eyes, it was getting light outside. He was lying on the floor, half-frozen and with broken bones. For a moment he wondered why on earth he had slept there. Then a headache and a look around reminded him why: Elijah was snoring in his bed, his belly full of his food and covered by his jacket and clean clothes. He still had his overalls on — and his face was covered in blood, he realized when he felt the skin under his nose and around his mouth pull. He thought it was a good time to take his hat back. He sat up, but at that slightest movement Elijah opened his eyes and looked at him, instantly awake.

"Hey, man, no hard feelings. You did it to yourself."

Daniel did not answer him, grim.

"When do they bring breakfast?" Elijah boldly asked..

"They don't bring it if you don't work."

"But you do work," Elijah commented casually.

"Count on it." Daniel, who could already feel his hands twitching, showed him his middle finger.

"Take your time."

Elijah turned away, going back to sleep.

Daniel went outside for a breath of calming air. *Maybe I'll kill him today*, he thought. What was certain was that the leech had to go. If he worked all morning carrying buckets, he would not have the strength to protect himself for lunch, and he was sure that Elijah would overpower him again without barely moving a finger. Besides, if he didn't work, he wouldn't have lunch anyway. Why the hell wasn't the sign guy fixing this?

He wandered around looking for Kitty; it had been a day since he had seen him. He certainly doesn't like the black man's presence, chuckled Daniel to himself. He was a clever beast; he was not his cat for nothing.

With a sluggish spirit he set to his usual work. He pulled the weeds and removed the pests from the leaves, examining them one by one. At first, those caterpillars that were so green they looked phosphorescent had grossed him out to no end. When he crushed them they squirted out a repulsive blue slime; they must have been alien caterpillars. If he didn't catch them in time, they were capable of laying a trillion eggs and gulping down an entire plant in no time. So he never hurried when he did that job. He had to be extra careful because, he didn't know how, someone after him would check and notice everything. The nagging thought of the guy sleeping in his bed, however, did not leave him alone and robbed him of his concentration. He had just resolved to go kick him awake when the guy popped out of the door stretching and yawning like a yeti.

"So, are we going to eat or not?"

"You have to get out of here. You're not getting anything."

"Yesterday I got plenty."

"Today is another day."

"We'll see."

The confidence he displayed was stinging. Daniel entered the hut to wash his hands in the bucket and found the other bucket full of piss.

"Hey," he made for the door toward Elijah. "I'm not emptying this – it's your stuff."

"Leave it there." Elijah shrugged, completely uninterested.

Daniel grabbed the bucket, determined to throw every last stinking drop of its contents into Elijah's face, but it would have soaked him in piss too. They stared into each other's eyes for an eternal instant, as in a Wild West duel. Each seemed to read and ponder the other's thoughts. Elijah knew that Daniel would not take a second longer to empty the bucket into his face. Then he would beat the shit out of him, sure, but let's just say that the idea of being showered with his own piss did not appeal to him. For his part, Daniel was now dead set on giving the guy a good bath in his own soup. He did not want to show that he was afraid, because that would be the end of him. Either he would try it now, or the black guy would take over forever, set up there and eat his food. He no longer wanted to feel the hunger tearing at his stomach. His body was still bruised from the punches of the day before, but he decided he would do as he always did; he would face up to even those stronger and bigger than him. Maybe he would have to take a beating, but under no circumstances would he back down. He would not give up; there was still the luck factor. And then courage was always appreciated, by people like Elijah. He made the gesture of lifting the bucket.

"Give me back my hat."

There can't be two taskmasters, they both thought simultaneously. Surprisingly, Elijah took off the hat and threw it at his feet.

"How long have you been here? And how did you get here?"

Sitting in front of the lit stove, they shared their food: a medium-sized fish, now made almost edible by recent practice. Once cleaned of what needed to be removed, though, there was almost nothing left. It was little for one, let alone two. Elijah had harvested two eggs and boiled them in a tin can over the fire. They were very good, they both agreed. *At least it contributed to the meal,* Daniel thought.

"And so, you've been here for you don't even know how long and you're banging away from dawn to dusk for a lousy can of broccoli," summed up Elijah with a wry grin that the other did not like at all. "And why would you do that, then?"

Daniel shrugged; he did not know. What was certain was that he had more or less gotten used to it and almost fit into that routine. However, he didn't want to tell that other guy there. He wouldn't understand anyway.

"But why don't you run away?"

"To go where?"

"I don't know. . . There must be an exit around here somewhere! I want to go back home, I mean," he rushed, "to my life. I'm not going to obey instructions on a paper hanging on the wall."

Daniel looked at him in disbelief; it was obvious that Elijah had no idea what that forest was. "And how would you go about leaving?" he challenged him.

"Well, in the meantime, I found you. Together we are stronger."

Daniel looked at the fire, absorbed; he wasn't sure he wanted to leave with this guy. And he certainly didn't feel stronger than when he had first arrived there. Physically he had grown, sure; he could do things that would have been unthinkable before. But as for ditching the bed and the safe meal to face the woods again, with the hunger, the darkness, the beasts, the noises – no, he wasn't going to make it.

"Which direction would you go?" He feigned interest.

"It's all the same. Sooner or later, somewhere, the forest has to end. There will be a road, a house with a telephone. . ."

"What if there isn't?"

"There is." Elijah stared straight into his eyes, menacingly. "And I'm not staying here."

Daniel continued to stare into the fire.

Suddenly they heard a long "Meeeooooowwww. . ." and he leapt to his feet. Kitty was back! He went to open the door as Elijah stared at him, amazed to see him suddenly so happy.

"Well?" he asked him.

"It's my cat," Daniel explained, letting him in.

When he saw the cat, Elijah burst out laughing to tears. Daniel did not understand.

"Hahaha! That's the ugliest cat I've ever seen!"

Kitty had a dead rat in his mouth and deposited it at the feet of Daniel, who felt almost moved by the gesture.

"Good Kitty, here," he whispered as he bent down to give him the entrails of the fish he had set aside for him, hoping to see him again.

"What a ridiculous critter," Elijah said again, wiping away his tears. Then he took a glowing stick from the stove's mouth and brought it close to the animal's fur.

"What are you doing?!" cried Daniel, pulling the cat toward him.

"Come on, let's see what he does!"

When Daniel realized that Elijah was not joking and really wanted to set Kitty's tail on fire, he was overwhelmed with anger. He would not have been as upset even if Elijah had offended his mother.

"Listen," he told him. "I'm staying here, I'm not going with you. But I really hope you find your way out."

Elijah looked at him incredulously. "I mean, you'd rather stay here slaving away with this sorry cat, eating a little lousy food?"

"Without me, you'll go faster, right?"

"You're out of your mind!" exclaimed Elijah with exaggerated contempt, because in reality he would never admit it but he wasn't sure he wanted to venture into the woods alone. He had spoken now, though, and he did not want to look like a coward. "And you're chickenshit, too."

"Think what you like." Daniel patted Kitty, sure he had made the right decision. He did not like being called chickenshit; in the past he would have raised his fists for much less. Now, however, he simply couldn't wait to get that creep out of his hair.

That night was terrible. Elijah took up Daniel's bed again, and although he was more than exhausted, he did not close his eyes. He did not trust him; he thought him capable of anything, even of setting fire to the hut with him in it, to persuade him to follow him or even just for spite or mischief. He closed his eyes as it began to dawn outside.

It's a good thing I kept my jacket on, or Elijah would have swiped that, too, was his first thought when he woke up with his still-broken bones and realized that he had had his hat robbed yet again. He felt like a real dope. Elijah was gone and the piss bucket was tipped onto the floor. The stench was nauseating. He would have to waste a lot of time making trips to get water to throw on the floor. He threw a couple of curses at the black man and hoped he would never see him again. He went outside; he was certain he would not find him. He looked around and indeed Elijah was no longer there. Daniel breathed a sigh of relief, then sat down on the doorstep. He was so tired. The sparse food and poor sleep had worn him out. He would never be able to work through the day, which would mean little food. He was depressed.

He was worse than depressed. He was still struggling with his imagination, which in moments of discouragement sadistically turned to images of plates of hamburgers and fries, when he heard a quick stomping behind him. He sprang to his feet. Perhaps he had been mistaken and it was Elijah, who had not really left. With a bound he was behind his shack. Pinned to the wooden wall, a white sheet of paper stood out.

YOUR WORK HERE IS DONE.
THANK YOU.

On the back of the sheet, there was another map.

PART TWO

DANIEL

Before leaving the shack, Daniel took one last look at "his" vegetable garden. He was a little sorry to leave it half-finished. He wouldn't have admitted it even under torture, but he had ultimately had a good experience in that place. He had poured a lot of time and sweat over that land. He had worked the field and, in some ways, the field had worked him. Before he had arrived, he would never have imagined toiling in that way and especially doing it obeying someone who did not even know what he looked like. Even his body had changed. Now he felt stronger, more resilient, almost more his own. And now that he had to put it all back on the line, a kind of anger came over him, with that new map in his hand that drew him away from what he had come to know, toward a novelty that he felt was hostile simply because it was new. Yet he was certain that if he did not follow the order, he would have to experience hunger again, and he remembered it all too well to want to face it again.

"Goodbye, cabbage. Someone else will eat you!" he said out loud, feeling like a bit of an imbecile talking to vegetables.

He had almost nothing to take with him. He made a ball out of his clean clothes, put his compass in one pocket and a full water bottle in the other. He studied the map for a while. He was beginning to know his surroundings and had learned how to orient himself. He had to follow an invisible path inside the forest to the X, but it was certainly easier to reach it by walking along the riverbanks than by having those ambiguous stylized drawings of rocks and trees as references. He was convinced that by doing it his way he would avoid getting lost and probably take less time as well.

"I'm going to the X," he said to himself, but as if addressed to the man who was forcing him there. "However, by the way I see fit. Let's go, Kitty!" He turned to the cat, who followed him as a dog would have done.

Daniel walked for quite a while; the road was level, but strewn with constant obstacles. Large stones, fallen tree trunks, and impassable bramble hedges forced him to stray far from the riverbed. Yet he kept telling himself that his path must be better than the one suggested by the map, because the sound of the river and the sense of the current acted as his sure guides.

He looked up at the sky. The sun was right at the peak of its path; it must be noon now. The somber rumbling of his stomach confirmed it. He had thought he would arrive earlier. Clearly, he had miscalculated the distance. He munched on the hard bread in his pocket, but his stomach, even though it had had to adjust to the new diet, was still used to more substantial food. This put him in a bad mood. The worst came when, after yet another detour, he came upon a sloping rock face several feet high. He stood staring at it for a long time, from bottom to top and back again; he had not anticipated it. He could not imagine that at some point the shore would be interrupted by that kind of perpendicular wall. He was not dumb enough to try to climb it; it was too steep, high, and slanted the wrong way. If he fell, he would be crushed.

Perhaps the more sensible thing would have been to go around it from the right, taking up the path the stranger had marked on the map. But apart from the fact that, at that point, he did not want to give in to him, it would have meant going quite a distance from where he was now. He would have wasted a lot of time and without the certainty of finding the right path again. The only sure thing was that he would spend the night in the middle of the woods. That was the last thing he wanted. Daniel racked his brain to come up with an alternative. The quickest way, though risky, was to cross to the left, into the water.

He took off his shoes, tied them by the laces, and hung them around his neck. He proudly noticed, trying to find it in himself to face that path through the water, that the repair to the boot he had had to make at the beginning of this whole thing still held up. The things he did, he could do well. He rolled up his pants and dipped his feet into the river; it was freezing, but the current did not seem too strong. He turned to look for Kitty and did not find him, so he was forced to get out of the water again, calling out to him. A furtive movement signaled his presence inside a bush.

"I know cats hate water," he chuckled, scooping him up and forcibly dragging him out, "but I promise you won't get a single hair wet!"

He grabbed him by the scruff of his neck and put him over one shoulder, like Long John Silver's parrot. As soon as he re-entered the water, Kitty dug her nails into his skin, through his shirt. "Hey!" he yelled at him, but he was too focused on watching where he put his feet.

The water was murky and the bottom could not be seen. Daniel proceeded slowly, clinging to the few handholds the rock wall offered, with the water now up to his belly. Kitty, fearing the worst, climbed up on his head, tearing at his hair.

It all happened in a flash; suddenly there was nothing under his feet, and Daniel ended up entirely under water. If there had been someone watching him, he would have seen for a few seconds the strange sight of a cat sitting on the water moving forward without lifting a paw.

Only after what seemed an interminable time, when he had no more breath in his lungs, did Daniel manage to return to the surface, fumbling for a handhold. Miraculously he found one and, terrified, holding on only with his arms, he returned the way he had already come, with the cat frozen on his head, stiff as if he were dead. When he felt the bottom under his feet again, he knew that he would survive.

Spitting up water and with his heart beating wildly, he threw himself onto the shore, breathing heavily. He struggled to get Kitty off his head; he did not trust him enough to let go. Effectively, though, Daniel had kept his word; he had not gotten a single hair wet.

Warm blood trickled down his temple. He gently swatted the cat, who cooperated and jumped down. They stared at each other for a moment with the same fear-filled gaze of one who has been within an inch of death and survived.

"Okay, I admit it," Daniel said, lying on his back and looking at the scraps of sky through the branches. "I don't know how to swim and I was dumb enough not to pay attention to the map. And then to try to go through there. . . ." He pointed to the placid water lapping at the base of the rock wall.

For a moment, he had been sure he was drowning; the water had become too deep and the current, stronger at that point, was literally sucking him in and dragging him away. He did not know what he had clung to either, perhaps a root or an underwater plant. I mean, it was a miracle. His clothes were all soaked, even his spare clothes. The map could barely be read, but Daniel remembered it by heart. It was clear to him that he had to turn around and start all over again from the hut, following the path marked by the stranger, who was leading him through the dense forest. In a black mood, angry at he knew not whom, he followed the course of the river back, retracing his steps, and by evening he was at "'home."

Distressed, hungry, covered in scratches and with sticky thorns covering him, he entered the shed, well aware that he would find the fire out. Worse, that he would have to face the night with the notorious hole in his belly. Kitty followed in dismay, dragging his paws as well. It had been a bad day.

Daniel squinted his eyes; the fire was lit and there was a can of chickpeas and fresh bread on the floor. It melted the knot in his throat and he felt his eyes become moist. He ran an arm over them and pulled up with his nose. In no way did he intend to cry, even though there were no witnesses. The truth was that he had been afraid that day, so damn afraid. For the first time, he had realized that he was not immortal and could get hurt and that if he died no one would know, no one would come looking for him. His body could have floated in the river until it decomposed, eaten by fish.

Instead, that unexpected fire and the food told him that someone was watching him, from not very far away, and that someone perhaps did not hate him, as he had first believed and, indeed, however rudely, even cared for him.

He remained seated in front of the fire, letting his clothes dry in the heat of the flames.

"We'll try again tomorrow," he told Kitty without taking his eyes off the stove. "But the right way."

He wrapped himself in the rough blanket and slept with the cat warming his belly.

Using the route indicated on the map, Daniel arrived in a single morning. As he had imagined, who knows why, since there was only an X on the map, he glimpsed a shack. It was bigger than the one he had lived in up to that point, though, and better kept.

"You can see that in this kind of survival game, when you pass a 'level,' you get 'bonuses,'" Daniel explained to Kitty.

For a moment, he felt like the cool star of a video game. Perfectly cast in character, he swung the door wide open with an aggressive kick.

"Didn't they teach you to knock?"

Daniel stood petrified in front of the open door, his mouth open wide in a dumbfounded expression that was anything but heroic. In front of him stood an old man, his pants down showing his pale legs and hideous yellowed knickers. Not at all perturbed, he finished dressing, fastened his pants and walked toward him.

"Now we'll do it again," he said, shutting the door unceremoniously in his face.

Daniel remained bewildered, arms along his sides, for almost two whole minutes. Then the door opened again and he found himself nose to nose with the old man, who explained himself better, speaking to him slowly as if he were a small child, or an idiot. " 'Now then . . . I'll close the door. You knock. You say, 'May I come in?' and I say, 'Come in.' And then, you enter."

Daniel couldn't believe his ears, and the old man slammed the door in his face for the second time.

Before all of this, he would have turned on his heels and walked away . . . after he'd sworn at the old man, which goes without saying. He was surprised that the anger was not rising, coursing to his fists, as it usually did; he stayed where he was.

His fist rose, but to knock, because, one: he didn't know where else to go, and two: the old man had completely bewildered him by the way he had addressed him. Generally, with him, adults always played the sweet-talk card, to soften him up. The teachers, his parents. . . But, for the record, it had not worked once. In fact, he would pull the string until it broke. He loved it when the teachers lost their temper and started yelling, so it became clear that they weren't perfect either. Daniel had a gift for bringing out the worst in people.

The old man in the shack, on the other hand, in just a few minutes, had slammed the door on his nose twice already, and openly treated him like a jerk. Daniel had not caught even a tinge of irony in that gesture or in his words; he could tell that he was not joking at all and made no effort to like him. In fact, he did not know why, but Daniel was sure that he already hated him. So he stayed, if only to watch and see what would happen.

"Come in," said the voice abruptly from inside the shed.

Daniel entered cautiously.

"That's better," the old man, who had his back to him from the rear of the room, said, without even turning to look at him, "but you didn't ask for permission."

You should talk while looking people in the face, Daniel said to himself, because the teachers in school always told him that. But the words to scold the old man in turn did not come out of his mouth.

"And you knocked a little too vigorously," the man continued, "but in a log cabin in the middle of the woods, it may be understandable."

The old man finished fixing something that Daniel could not see, because he insisted on having his back to him.

"By the way, I am Peter. I live here. You will stay with me. That's your bed," he said, pointing to a cot in the corner. "And now, I'm going fishing." He grabbed a rod and a net and made to leave.

"What about me?" asked Daniel, increasingly bewildered.

Was he supposed to live with this madman? And for how long? He had fallen out of favor with the game.

"Right," the old man remembered. "They left something for you," and with his head he motioned to a large yellow envelope on the table.

"'They' who? Who left it?"

But Peter walked out without looking back, ignoring him completely and slamming the door behind him. Daniel approached the table and picked up the envelope. He walked over to the window and looked at it against the light; it looked empty. He opened it and pulled out a folded sheet of paper. Two photos slid to the floor at his feet. One pictured him at age six, with his mother, on the first day of elementary school. In the other he was in his father's arms, before a Halloween party, dressed as an astronaut. What was he supposed to do with those pictures? He opened the paper and recognized the usual handwriting.

PLEASE OBSERVE.

Something inside him rebelled against the task. He had no intention of carrying out this stupid order, if possible even stupider than digging thousands of stones out of the vegetable garden.

He threw the pictures on the table and went out in search of the old man. Where had he gone fishing? It could not have been very far. He spotted a path in the greenery and followed it. He found himself, after a quick descent, on the riverbank. Peter, motionless, almost one with the boulder on which he was sitting, stared attentively at the water. He approached him, but the man blatantly ignored him, almost ridiculously so, considering that they were probably the only two human beings within miles. Daniel stood for a long time watching, but nothing was happening. When he made to open his mouth, the old man scolded him, muttering with a straw between his teeth. "Shut up; you'll scare the fish away."

Daniel closed his mouth again. Part of him wanted to leave right away, screaming purposely to scare even the last stinking fish and ruin the outing for that obnoxious old man. Instead, the other side won, the side that absolutely wanted to stay and see if anything came up. He had never been fishing in his life and might even have liked it.

He sat on the grass looking ostentatiously in another direction, so as not to show the old man that he was interested in what he was doing. He was actually peeking out of the corner of his eye all the time, but the guy wasn't paying attention to him at all. He just stared fixedly at the water, caught up in his thoughts, as if Daniel wasn't even there.

After quite a while, he fumbled to pull a white wrapper out of a vest pocket. It took Daniel three seconds to figure out what it was, and he began to salivate when he saw, poking out of the wrapper, just what he had imagined: a giant sandwich. The old man bit into it, chewing slowly and accompanying each bite with an exaggerated sigh of satisfaction. An unspeakable anger came over Daniel; why had he always been told in his life that one should share one's belongings with others, while this guy ate without offering him anything? Not that he had ever learned that lesson; the most he had shared in the past had been cigarettes, and he had only given them to those he knew would reciprocate. But all the old man's sighs, the relaxed biting of a sandwich that he would devour in 30 seconds flat. . . He had the impression that he was doing it on purpose, and it infuriated him. Hunger was blinding him, and he hadn't eaten a sandwich in ages.

Just for an instant, he imagined sneaking up behind the old man, snatching the sandwich from him, and knocking him out of the way by shoving him into the water. However, he didn't even have time to get to his feet when, with horror, he witnessed the guy crumble what was left of the sandwich and throw it into the water to the fish. Anger gave way to despair. As if suddenly remembering him, Peter cast him a quick glance.

"It's called baiting," he explained to him. "It's to attract fish."

Daniel cursed him with his thoughts. What did he care about the fish? He wanted the sandwich. Besides, they had been there for hours and not a damn thing was biting. Fishing was the most boring sport in the world, even worse than golf. He was about to leave, when, unexpectedly, the float disappeared underwater and the rod bent until it almost broke. The old man, who, up to that point, had seemed half asleep, sprang to his feet grabbing the rod with two hands and giving a tug. The fish was pulling like hell, and Peter gave it some line and then, drawing the rod to himself and turning the reel, brought it back. Daniel had no idea what was under the surface of the water, but it had to be big and determined to live. He watched the line dart left and right and saw the clear concentration with which the old man loosened and pulled. As he watched him, mesmerized, after standing up, he felt a kind of excitement growing inside. He hated the old man, but he hoped he would win over the fish, because he really wanted to see how big that sucker was.

When Peter finally managed to pull it out of the water, Daniel's eyes widened. The fish, glistening in the sun, seemed to be made of silver, and wriggled like a maniac to free itself. It was truly gigantic and almost pitiful, so powerful and already doomed.

"What are you doing, standing there staring?" the old man abruptly awakened him. "Hurry up and hand me the net," he ordered, as he continued to pull. Daniel complied without taking his eyes off the prey, stretching as much as he could and trying not to end up in the water. With difficulty, he caught it with the net and laid it on a rock.

"Good," commented Peter dryly, finishing the fish with a sharp jab and putting the net and rod over his shoulder. "So we're eating today."

He started toward the cabin without saying a word to Daniel. *Not even a thank you*, he thought. The guy really was the rudest adult he had ever met. He seemed to have forgotten all about him again, now that he no longer needed his help. In fact, he went into the house and slammed the door in his face. Overlooking that umpteenth rudeness, Daniel followed him inside. It didn't seem like the time to be too fancy; it must have been two o'clock in the afternoon, and Daniel was blindly hungry. Until that moment he had chewed only anger. He watched Peter gut the fish with a quick, skillful move and set it to cook on the stove. It was clear that he knew what he was doing, for the food gave off a delicious smell, quite different from the fish that Daniel usually charred on his own stove, although, he would have bet, the breed was the same. Lunch sizzled in butter and Daniel's mouth was already watering when, with genuine horror, he saw Peter put it on one plate and begin to eat.

"What about me?" he asked for the second time that morning. "I helped you, too!"

The old man looked up from his plate with a face that was just asking to be smacked. "Did you do your homework?" he asked him with his mouth full. You could tell from his tone that he didn't care about the answer at all.

What the f—- kind of question was that? He had been with him the whole time! He knew full well that he hadn't done anything. Besides, what the hell homework was he talking about?

"What homework?"

"The one in the envelope."

"Looking at two pictures? Of course I looked at them. It's not like I'm an idiot."

The old man was definitely getting on his nerves.

"And what would you have seen?" asked Peter as he continued eating.

Daniel knew for sure that if he did not answer, that guy would finish the rest of the fish in two bites.

"There's me as a kid with my parents," he replied quickly.

Peter looked him straight in the eye. "That's it?"

"That's all," insisted Daniel nervously.

The old man continued to chew noisily in silence. Then he licked his fingertips with pleasure and willful slowness, one by one, producing unbearable pops. He's doing this on purpose to annoy me, Daniel convinced himself.

"You didn't look properly," he finally told him, getting up from the table and throwing himself on the bed. "Now I'm going to take a nap. You see that you do your homework well if you want to eat dinner," and at a speed that wasn't even human, he closed his eyes and almost instantly began snoring.

Daniel was starving, and exhaustion seared his brain. He picked up the pictures again and stared at them with hatred. What? What was he supposed to see in those faded pieces of paper? He didn't want to look at them. They couldn't force him!

He shifted over to the patched cabinet by the door. He was certain that canned food supplies were hiding behind the doors. He opened them, trying to be as quiet as possible, and then exulted; he had guessed right! He reached out to take what was rightfully his – or at least, that's how he justified it to himself – but before taking a can he instinctively turned to check that the old man was still asleep.

Peter's gaze, fixed on him, had the power to freeze him.

"You haven't worked," Peter told him as he remained lying down. "You cannot eat."

"I'm hungry; I'm going to eat," Daniel communicated to him in response. He rebelliously felt like he was before an adult again, and especially with an adult like him, he felt the worst part of himself coming out once more.

With a quick and unexpected burst, Peter leapt out of bed and in an instant was close to him. Daniel did not retreat; he stared him straight in the eyes, clutching the can of chickpeas in his hand. The old man was tall, much taller than Daniel was, and perhaps not as old as he had seemed at first.

"Maybe I didn't make myself clear. Put that can down," he said glacially.

Click.

With a gesture of defiance Daniel snapped the lid ring and began to open the can.

It was swift and painful, the slap that Peter dealt him right in the face. His hand was rough and heavy and seemed to be made of wood. With his cheek throbbing, Daniel was blind with rage. No adult, not even his father, had ever laid a hand on him. And although he had taken a lot in fights at school, no blow had ever hurt him like that slap.

He raised his arm to hit him back.

"Don't you dare," the old man warned him coldly and menacingly, as he grabbed his arm in midair in a most painful grip. With his other hand, he grasped him by the shirt and literally lifted him off the ground, bringing his face closer to his own. His breath smelled fishy and his eyes drilled into his brain.

"I'm not like others you've known, kid. Don't ever try that again, or you won't even have time to regret it."

There was a kind of mad, determined light at the bottom of his gaze. And also something akin to a fierce and unyielding sorrow, a regret driven like a rusty nail into the old man's chest. It goes without saying that Daniel was afraid. He did not doubt for a moment that the man could beat him, and badly.

"Do you understand?" Peter shook him as if he were a puppet.

Daniel did not respond. The old man shook him again, harder. "Yes or no?"

"Yes," Daniel replied through clenched teeth.

The man seemed to suddenly calm down; his eyes became dull again, his hand let go of his grip.

"Then go do what you have to do," and he went back and flopped on the bed, falling fast asleep.

This is totally insane, thought Daniel. *Why did they put me with this madman? I'm leaving now.*

Instead, he stood and watched the old man sleeping with his back to him. He was sure he would not be able to catch him off guard if he approached him. Perhaps as a young man he had been a soldier. Certainly he was some kind of caveman. He was old, but still very strong. He had lifted him two feet off the ground and shaken him like a rag doll. *Maybe as a kid he had been tough like me*, Daniel told himself again. Maybe he, too, had been someone who had never listened to anyone saying things like: "Look people in the face when you talk," "Offer others a snack if they don't have one," "Say thank you if someone helps you." Whatever. It was obvious that he made his own rules. He had ended up living alone in a cabin in the middle of the woods; he had probably found no one who could stand him. Yet . . . he seemed to need nothing, confident enough to feel no desire for the approval of others. How skillfully he had pulled up that whale of a thing earlier at the river! Daniel would have loved to have known how to fish like that. And never have to say thank you to anyone. Then, he noticed the photos on top of the table. He shook off all those useless thoughts and listlessly sat down to look at them.

He vividly remembered the first day of elementary school, 11 years earlier, even though a lot of time had passed. His mother had bought him new overalls. The backpack, on the other hand, was used, but it looked almost new, too; it had robots on it. In the picture, he was smiling. Of course I was, he said to himself, because I didn't know what was in store for me yet. The teacher had yelled at him all the time because he couldn't sit for more than 10 minutes straight. It had been so boring, as well as irritating. The other children had teased him because he had bread and cheese for snack. One had started saying that he smelled like a goat, and the others had followed suit.

Even his mother, in the picture, was smiling. That day, who knows how many expectations she had for him. Poor thing! You could see she was proud and even a little tense, yet happy. There were no pictures of the second day of school, and that was good. Daniel was sure his mother would never look like that again. He had gotten his first teacher's note; he had shoved the boy who kept saying he smelled like a goat.

He was reminded of the afternoon not long before his current trial when he had hit his mother and felt strange. Eleven years had passed since the picture was taken and she had aged as if it was twice as long. The worries he caused her and the strain of work had sucked the youth out of her. It could not have been easy for her to leave her country, her family... and build a new life in a place whose language she did not even speak. It was the first time he had stopped to think about it. Once, as a child, he too had been to Romania and understood why Mom had left. When he felt a kind of lump rise in his throat, he took the other picture between his fingers.

He was on his father's lap. His dad had made the astronaut suit for him out of cardboard from supermarket boxes. It was a respectable Space Ranger suit – his father had a way with cardboard and colors. Daniel, very proud, had gone to school imagining the faces of the others upon seeing him walk in like that. But his classmates, all wearing the same Spider-Man costume, had teased him again and ripped his suit to shreds in front of the teacher. She had not moved a finger and had stood by and watched. Not a single rebuke had come out of her mouth. And although a lot of time had passed, Daniel still felt all the anger and bitterness of that time because he was aware, and was aware even at six years old, that what his classmates had done to him was not right and that it was even less right that the teacher had not defended him. He was sure she had not said anything because, from her point of view, that costume made by his daddy was not worth anything, because it was just a piece of cardboard covered with tinfoil. It had not cost money, it had not been bought in a store.

So Daniel had come to his own aid. The punch with which he had made his point was more than justified, but it had been a little too hard. The other child's nose had begun to bleed, so the teacher had woken up and intervened, rushing in to grab him by the ear. He remembered, as if it was in front of his eyes now: the humiliation his father had suffered when he had had to apologize to his classmate's dad, who had treated him terribly. He had not liked seeing him so bent out of shape. He didn't even like remembering that scene now. Still, what a happy face she had in that picture, with him on her lap... *Because even when things look good,* Daniel thought, *we never know what awaits us next. Reality always disappoints. People always disappoint. I always disappoint others. Even when I don't want to.*

He turned the pictures face down on the table so he would never have to see them again. They caused a sharp pain in his chest. He realized that he missed his mother, and he did not like that the last things he remembered about his father were his harsh words and angry face when he had thrown him out of the car. If he had a phone, maybe he would have called them.

With surprise, he discovered that it was getting dark outside. His belly growled; his head ached from hunger. He heard Peter getting out of bed. He had almost forgotten about him. He saw him pick up the cauldron full of water that was always ready by the fire, put it on top, and pour a whole package of pasta into it without even waiting for it to boil. After a short while, surprisingly, the old man ladled it onto his plate, pushing it closer to him to invite him to eat. He was not one of many words. Daniel did not let the quiet invitation be repeated twice.

They ate in silence with the fire crackling and their jaws working.

"Well?" questioned Peter, staring at him grimly, as if waiting for something.

"Thanks for dinner," muttered Daniel, hoping he had gotten the right answer right.

Then Peter pulled his chair over to the fireplace and started reading a book. Daniel stood watching him for a while. With the book in his hand and his brow furrowed in concentration, he looked like a different person. It occurred to Daniel that perhaps, in the past, the old man had been more than just a soldier. He found the courage to speak. "Can I ask you a question?"

"If it's really necessary," he grunted as he continued reading.

"You're a teacher, aren't you?"

Peter's mouth pulled into a kind of smile, disguised behind a grimace. "What makes you think that?"

"Sixth sense," Daniel replied, remaining vague.

"Retired," Peter clarified, moistening his index finger and turning the page.

So he had got it right: Peter had been a teacher. In his day, he must have terrorized quite a few pupils, poor things. He couldn't see him being nice at all, as his teachers tried to be to him.

"What are you reading?" he asked, even though he didn't care at all. He had been silent for too long and felt like talking, even if it was about books and with that species of Bigfoot, Peter.

"Stuff you wouldn't understand."

Daniel felt stung, taking a real interest now. ""How would you know?" he asked hotly. Why did everyone who saw him, without even knowing him, have to call him stupid? Did he have it written on his forehead?

"Because you can't even distinguish east from west," clarified Peter. But seeing Daniel's face, he softened. "Anyway – everything in its own time." He closed the conversation and the book and began fiddling with the fishing pole.

"Can I go to the river with you tomorrow?" asked Daniel, trying not to sound pleading.

"It's not up to me. You have to finish your task first."

"But I did. And that's dumb."

"Then it means you didn't understand, so you have to continue. Good night," the old man dismissed him permanently.

Daniel threw himself onto his cot. The anger welling up inside him prevented him from sleeping for a long time.

He spent an entire week devoting himself to that stupid task. By now he knew every detail of those photos by heart. He noted the time marked by the kitchen clock on the wall behind him, the number of buttons his overalls had, the title of the TV program magazine resting on the table next to his father – all seemingly insignificant details, but instead they had served to open wide the doors of memory for him.

The magazines had disappeared from his house the first time his father had lost his job, along with the television and all the other things considered superfluous. He lost at least one button a day, and his mother always scolded him because buttons cost money. Yet she had never sent him to school without a button. Besides, there was only one set of overalls, and it needed to be washed, dried and ironed in a hurry every Sunday so that it would be ready again by Monday. He had never realized the sacrifices and renunciations his parents made for him until he held the pictures in his hands and was forced to look at them for hours. The clock also brought to his mind another detail: the first day of elementary school had been the only one on which he had arrived on time. As early as the second day, he had begun to throw a tantrum because he did not want to go; school had immediately been a nightmare for him and for his mother.

That thought had released others, and Daniel was buried by memories of all the times he had disappointed his parents or angered them. You couldn't count them all. He had made their lives hell. And for what, then?

So?" asked Peter one evening after dinner.
"So what?" Daniel looked at him questioningly.
"So, what conclusion have you come to?"
Daniel finally grasped at an answer.
"That I'm an asshole."
"Well, to realize that is something. To admit it so sincerely, then, is heroic."
Peter was being serious, but Daniel couldn't tell if he was making fun of him. As always, he saw him finish his dinner and sit down with his book in front of the fire. It was his turn to clear the table and wash the dishes. He got it done in a few minutes. He felt a great desire to talk, but in all that time Peter had given him little satisfaction. He sat down next to him, but he, as he always did, ignored him. Daniel was not discouraged.

"What did you teach when you were young?"

Peter did not even take his eyes off the pages.

"Private banking."

Daniel had no idea what that was. Certainly not something taught in a vocational school; it had to be hard stuff. He looked for an intelligent question.

"And in which high school?"

Peter looked at him in amazement for a moment before bursting out laughing in his face. "Ha ha!" He wiped a tear from one eye. "I needed a good laugh," he said, catching his breath. Then, becoming more serious, "We really need to cure you of this ignorance of yours."

Daniel took great offense and Peter explained himself better.

"You can't come back into the world and make such an impression."

"The people I hang out with don't talk about this stuff,'" he sulked.

"Then maybe you should hang out with other people. The ones who make you better."

Okay, thought Daniel resentfully and angrily, *it's impossible to talk to the old man. He is exactly like all the other teachers; born to make you feel like shit.*

He made to get up but, surprisingly, Peter started talking again. "Anyway, you don't study to put on airs or to have something clever to say. You study because it is good to learn and understand the world."

This time, it was Daniel who burst out laughing. "You sound just like a teacher! What do they give you in school, a book of catchphrases good for all students?"

Now, that was a smart thing to say.

"Yeah," the old man unexpectedly agreed with him without flinching at all, "That's why I don't like to talk.

120

Between people like us, it's almost impossible to understand each other." And he went back to reading.

Daniel felt terrible about this comment. What did he mean? Certainly, something negative. He stood for a while, hoping that the old man would add something else, like an explanation, or maybe an apology. But he remained immersed in his book. When he began to feel like a fool for standing there waiting for no one knew what, he emphatically said good night and went to sleep. He struggled like hell to get to sleep; he felt within himself a great need to get out and run. He had too much energy inside, which he had stifled for too long to go along with that absurd request to sit for hours staring at two pictures.

I'm about to burst, was his last thought.

The next day, there was a new yellow envelope on the table with his name written on it. Peter, who had woken him up by whistling, was warming breakfast.

Suspiciously, Daniel stared at the book resting under the letter. He recognized it very well; it was his science book. It really was his copy, confirmed by the scribbles he had made on it one dull morning when he was feeling particularly creative.

"Barley water and dry bread; the best breakfast ever," Peter said with unusual good humor, setting the two cups down on the table.

He observed Daniel, who stood looking at the letter and book as if they were explosive bombs.

"Well? Aren't you going to open the envelope?"

"I already know what's in it."

WELL DONE, THANK YOU.
STUDY, PLEASE.

121

"I knew it."

He showed Peter the letter.

He felt angry. Hoeing had seemed less tiring to him than studying. At least he was outside all day and then, at night, he was tired, but he felt good. Instead, studying was just a pain in the ass.

"What I haven't told you yet," Peter said with a half smile, "is that if you do what you have to in the morning, you can come with me in the afternoon."

"How do you know?"

"I just know."

Daniel thought about it for a while. The exchange seemed fair to him. Anything to get out of there.

"Okay."

Peter, already standing in the doorway with the fishing pole in hand, turned to look at him and, as if reading his mind, suggested, "Nothing forbids you to study outside." Then he went out.

Daniel, as disgusted as if he were handling a pair of underwear that was not his own, took the book and went out into the open air. Sitting on the ground he began to leaf through it listlessly, keeping it resting on a rock. *I don't have to go in order*, he thought; *the paper didn't say to do that.* He chose the page with the pictures he liked best. Kitty popped up from behind the shack. Daniel had the impression that he was keeping away from Peter – he always waited until he was gone to come out. *Maybe he doesn't like me either,* Daniel thought.

"The Solar System," he read aloud to Kitty, who stared at him as impassively as a sphinx.

He ran his eyes over two lines, then a little bird landed just a few steps away and he watched it hop. Kitty moved and the bird flew away. Daniel followed it with his eyes until it disappeared into the branches of a tree. His eyes then glanced up at the sky; it was crisscrossed by clouds. One looked just like an old woman on a motorcycle. He burst out laughing and continued playing with their shapes for along while.

When he lowered his eyes back to the book, the pages were reverberating with sunlight and reading them was annoying. He flipped through again, looking at the figures. They were beautiful; there were pictures of colored balls. Planets, he told himself. He couldn't tell one from the other and the explanations under the pictures were daunting, written too small. They did not persuade him to go deeper. It went on like this all morning. He noticed a squirrel jumping among the branches. All of a sudden, he even seemed to hear distinctly, carried from far away on the wind, the bleating of sheep. Kitty made his own contribution to the distraction by rubbing against his thigh, and then Daniel picked up a blade of grass and played with it.

It was a decent morning until Peter returned and Daniel remembered. He had not done his duty; would he eat? He looked worriedly at the two beautiful fish in the net. He entered the house behind him, forgetting the book outside.

So?" Peter questioned him as he cleaned the fish on the sink. "What did you learn that was good?"

Daniel felt as he did when they questioned him in school and he never knew anything. He did not answer.

"Then tell me what you learned the hard way," Peter joked.

"That you can't study outside."

Peter turned to look at him uncomprehendingly, and Daniel explained that too many things had distracted him: the cat, the clouds, the little bird. . . .

"What kind of bird?" asked Peter.

Daniel looked at him, astonished. Why didn't he scold him? What did he care about what kind of bird it was?

"How should I know?" he replied. "Just a little bird."

"Get that green book there," he pointed with his head to one of the seven books on the shelf above his bed, "and look it up."

Daniel flipped through the pages; they were filled with pictures of birds. He looked for a long time.

"There it is!" he exulted, as if he had discovered America.

"What is it?"

"Bull. . . finch," he read. "A bullfinch!"

He looked at the other photographs. "What other birds are around here?" he asked, for the first time in his life with curiosity.

"Several. You can take my binoculars, if you want, to-morrow afternoon. Maybe you can spot the hoopoe. It is a beautiful bird that loves absolute silence and lonely places."

Daniel looked for the hoopoe in the book and mean-while Peter put the plate in front of him. Daniel looked at it and then at him, as if asking permission.

"You will study this afternoon." It was not a polite in-vitation, but a politely expressed order.

"All right," Daniel said. It was fair. It was the deal.

He ate and after lunch he was alone in the house, sit-ting at the table studying. But how much did he have to study? One chapter? Two? It was a moot point; after the first five lines, he already had a headache and had to re-read again, because he did not understand anything. He reread. Nothing. He punched his head a couple of times to make the words fit better. All to no avail; he could not even memorize them. I'm stupid, he concluded. But he already knew this.

When Peter returned, he found him hunched over the book, his face all red with angry tears in his eyes.

"I tried," he defended himself, gritting his teeth. "I swear I tried, but I'm dumb." He settled a fist on his head.

"All right. I believe you. I'll help you tomorrow. Let's have dinner now."

And, for the second time that day and in his life, Daniel felt that he had stolen what he ate.

"Come with me," Peter said after dinner, getting up from the table and putting on his jacket to leave.

Daniel imitated him, amazed at this novelty. Peter had a flashlight. There was no moon in the sky, so it was pitch black, like the first night he had been abandoned in the woods. He recognized the dark sounds of animals, and if the old man had not been there, he would have been afraid.

"That is an owl," he explained to him when what sounded like a woman's cry rose from somewhere in the trees.

So it had been an owl that had terrorized him on nights when he had been alone. He had been frightened by a bird; he would never tell anyone outside the woods about it. The owl screeched again. *It makes a horrible noise, though*, Daniel justified himself, quickening his pace so as not to lose sight of Peter in the dark.

They were climbing; the invisible path through the bushes was very steep and rough. Daniel wondered how the old man could proceed with such confidence, while he was out of breath and his legs were wobbly from the climb. When he was beginning to see strange lights flashing before his eyes from the effort, Peter stopped. Daniel looked around, catching his breath. They were in an open space. Abruptly, the brush ended at a kind of promontory, bald as an old man's head, at the foot of which the river could be heard flowing. "Perfect evening," observed Peter, sitting down on the ground. After standing beside him, Daniel followed his gaze and looked up.

He was literally crushed by the vault of heaven. Everything was black up there, but there were so many stars that you couldn't count them. He was sure that in the city all this was not there. Or maybe it was, but it was hidden by the fog and the lights from the stores. He stood with bated breath, not knowing what to say. If the Hunchback had been there with him, he would have played his usual part, shrugging his shoulders and saying, "So what?"

But the Hunchback was not there and the old man was, which changed everything.

Daniel looked up again, his mouth open.

"Yeah," Peter said, reading his mind. "It does that to me, too."

"The brain is like a muscle; it has to be trained, or else it atrophies," said Peter sternly, as if this were the judgment of a neurosurgeon.

The expression on his face did not give much away, but to Daniel he seemed to be annoyed. He didn't even look like the same person as the night before, the one who had even almost smiled, looking up at the stars. Daniel could read his mind: he was wondering if that blockhead really was incapable of understanding the meaning of five lines. No, Daniel told himself dejectedly, I am not able, even though I have read them a hundred times.

"Let's do this," proposed the old man, "I'll read and you listen."

It went better. If he closed his eyes and could concentrate, and made an effort to grasp the meaning of the sentences by going beyond the empty sound of individual words, he seemed to understand better.

"Now tell me what you understood."

Daniel opened his mouth, convinced he could say something, but instead nothing came to him. He was sure he had caught something, but the words were not coming out.

Peter took his face in his hands and looked at him as if to study him, as if he were a rare animal.

"All right." He got up from the table. "Get the binoculars and come with me." Daniel followed him with no idea where they were going.

Peter moved securely through the brambles, following a path through the woods visible only to him. With a stick used as a machete, he was whipping blows left and right to clear the vegetation and create a gap where they could pass. Daniel, in turn, took a stick and wrestled with the brambles, as if they were giant enemies. The good thing was that he could hit them full force without doing much damage or getting hurt. He let off steam that way, enjoying himself like a child, until the old man began to climb up the trunk of a large tree.

Camouflaged among the leaves, high up, was a platform. Daniel climbed up too. It was not too stable and creaked with every movement. Seeing that Peter sat down, he did the same.

Then the old man, with his eyes glued to the binoculars, began scanning the trees. A very rapid drumming sound brought a smile to his face.

"I knew you were there," whispered Peter to himself. "Did you hear that?" he turned to Daniel.

"Of course! What was that?"

"Definitely a great spotted woodpecker. Where do you think the noise came from?"

"From over there," answered Daniel confidently, and Peter peered in that direction.

"Gotcha! See if you can spot it," he said, and handed him the binoculars. "It's black and white, with a red undertail."

It took Daniel a long time, but he had no intention of giving up.

"There it is!" he exulted.

Peter smiled at his sincere reaction. " Well done!" he praised him. "Do you hear that?"

A festive chirp rose up right next to them.

"It's two robins conversing with each other," he explained. "These birds are very trusting toward humans, not afraid to approach."

"Is one of them the bird over our head?" asked Daniel, lowering his voice so as not to startle him. With the binoculars it was like having it in front of his nose.

"Yes."

"It's easy to recognize him," Daniel observed, giving himself the air of a great expert.

"Legend has it that the robin's feathers are colored like that because he pulled out a thorn from Christ's crown to relieve his suffering and a drop of His blood fell on his chest, dying it red."

"Yeah, whatever," Daniel cut him short with condescension.

"I told you it's a legend, you jackass. Listen to me when I talk to you." Peter's professorial side had come out. "And by the way, if you're interested in scientific information, robins use ants to clean their feathers."

"Come on! What a story!"

"Yeah, he catches them with his beak and rubs them on his feathers."

"He basically uses them like a washcloth."

"That's right, because ants release formic acid, which disinfects and keeps pests away. It's called anting."

"In fact ant-man is ant man! But how does the robin know this?"

Peter did not comment on that last sentence and merely gave half a smile.

They went on for a good two hours with the birds, and Daniel was not bored for a moment. Once home, indeed, he took the book and went over the names of the species they had seen. Peter questioned him disinterestedly, and Daniel answered casually. He remembered everything.

At dinnertime, he froze on his feet as he set the table.

"We forgot to study!"

At home, he always happened to "forget" that he had homework, but this time he had a worried look on his face. Dinner came to his mind; perhaps he should have set the table for one?

"And what, in your opinion, do you think we have done so far?"

Daniel gasped, then the answer came naturally to him. "But it's not like we study birds in school."

"They are studied, all right," Peter contradicted him. "Did you notice that you remembered everything I told you today, word for word?"

"Of course, I'm not dumb!" defended Daniel as if it were a matter of course.

"I, in fact, never said that."

They dined in silence. For the first time, it seemed to Daniel that he had done something right and, what's more, something difficult. The old man, for his part, kept a placid demeanor. Daniel would rather get himself killed than admit that he was happy with how this day went, he thought, staring at his companion furtively. Yet he was convinced that somewhere beneath Peter's stony face, he hid a sliver of pride in how Daniel had remembered each of the explanations he had given him.

For a good week, without even batting an eye, Daniel listened to Peter talk about the respiratory and circulatory systems of birds, pneumatic bones, grain-eating and fruit-eating animals, molting, and the difference between winter plumage and summer mating plumage. He was astounded when Peter explained to him the behavior of carrier pigeons, especially when he told him about Frederick II and the treatise on falconry. The old man even went so far as to read him some poems and stories featuring birds, and Daniel found himself curious about their endings. On his own initiative, he read a good half of the bird book, and, when he did not understand something, he asked Peter. Effortlessly he remembered names and characteristics of species and even began to recognize the species when he saw or heard them, or from the nests he found around.

Peter's lessons did not stop with birds. Day after day, Daniel learned how to fish and how to recognize fish; how to set a line and how to overcome the disgust of hooking worms, if one wanted to catch worthwhile prey. And before that, worms had to be unearthed underground and caught with the hands feeling that rubbery, moist texture they had. While he was at it, Peter also explained to him the structure of ringworms, and Daniel listened open-mouthed to even the most absurd things, such as that worms have five hearts, which are fake hearts, however, and that it is not true that if you cut them in half they continue to live. He drank in every syllable of his explanations because these words were no longer abstract concepts, but living beings all too real in his hands. When Peter later found out that Daniel could not swim, he was literally horrified.

"What if you fall into a river?"

"There are no rivers in the city," Daniel defended himself.

"But there is one out front," Peter corrected him. "You never know what life has in store for you. . ."

Daniel shrugged. "I'm not stupid enough to fall into it," he sarcastically remarked. Kitty wasn't there and even if he had been, he couldn't have contradicted him.

"And if you go to the beach, what do you do? Sunbathe?"

"I've never been to the sea. My parents don't have enough money and they work all year round." He did not want to make the usual ignorant impression by asking him what sunbathing was.

Peter looked at him in a way he did not like, as if he was feeling sorry for him.

"Well, what is it?" asked Daniel, piqued. "A lot of people have never seen the sea."

Peter was silent for a moment.

"Yes, but there is a big difference between those who have seen it at least once and those who have never seen it."

"You are totally crazy." Daniel wanted to end that uncomfortable conversation as soon as possible.

"Get into your underwear," the old man suddenly ordered.

Daniel's eyes widened; perhaps he hadn't understood correctly.

"You can't swim with your clothes on," Peter explained.

Without knowing how or why, Daniel went along with him and found himself in his underwear. Peter forced him down into the icy river water to at least learn how to float. Daniel would never admit to anyone, and especially to him, that he was terrified of ending up submerged like the last time. He shuddered, but did not utter a single cry. He could tell from Peter's face that this was a big deal.

It took all the old man's stubbornness and Daniel's stubbornness to come to terms with it; terror made him deaf to the old man's instructions and heavy as an iron. "Stamp your feet!" the one shouted to him from the bank, but all he heard, since he was constantly going underwater with his head, was "St ... our .. eet!"

I won't quit for anything in the world, he told himself with a watered-down brain. That damn water was getting into him from every orifice, and one could certainly not learn to swim by keeping his ears and nose plugged. Eventually, almost on instinct, if only not to freeze to death, he began desperately moving his arms and legs and found himself floating like a cork. The old man did not even give him the satisfaction of a "bravo," but his face was worth a thousand compliments.

For every new thing he learned, Daniel felt stronger and more confident. He certainly would never talk birds with the Hunchback (who at most would stone pigeons), nor would he compete in swimming with any of his friends, nor even see the sea. Still, it was just as Peter had told him in the beginning; it was good to just know those things, even if maybe it was all useless stuff that would never serve him in life.

One evening, after dinner, Peter came out with one of his trademark phrases: "And now we come to the Solar System."

"Now?" Daniel yawned.

He had swam for an hour that morning and fished, too. He had spent the afternoon perched on a branch looking for the hoopoe, without success. He looked forward to bedtime.

"Let's go, come on." Peter would accept no objections.

They returned to the top of the rocky bluff.

"See that white ribbon of stars? Use your peripheral vision," he suggested.

"Yes, it looks like some kind of road."

"That's right. In fact, it's called the Milky Way. We're in there."

"I don't understand," Daniel yawned again, unable to concentrate. "If we are here, how can we be up there?"

"We are on Earth, which belongs to the Solar System, which is inside a galaxy called the Milky Way."

"It's too difficult for me," he said, trying to wash his hands of it.

Worms and birds were something he could understand, because they were there, within reach. As for swimming, even dogs could do it. But the stars, no, they were too far away from him, in every sense of the word.

"Yeah. You're right. Right now you're sitting on a ball of rock traveling at 1000 miles a minute. And whether you know it or not, you are always spinning."

"Wait, what's the story?" Finally, Daniel had fallen into the trap set by Peter. So he was on a spinning ball all the time?

"Besides," Peter continued, not paying attention to his question, "they may seem like abstract and distant things to you, but you and a star are ultimately made of the same stuff."

"That is, I would be made of light?" joked Daniel.

Peter stared at him seriously. "Sort of," he nodded, "In a way."

They remained silent, each chasing their own thoughts.

"But," Daniel observed, "sometimes it's nice just to look, without having to necessarily name everything."

Words often make even the simplest things difficult, he thought.

"You are getting wise," Peter said with his gaze fixed on the sky. Then he closed his eyes and began to recite what sounded like a poem:

"When I see your heavens, the work of your fingers, the moon and stars that you set in place — What is man that you are mindful of him, and a son of man that you care for him? Yet you have made him little less than the angels. . ."

After a long pause, Peter took a deep breath and opened his eyes again.

"Compared to the stars, what are we? Nothing. Yet, with thought, we can understand them and become great."

He turned to Daniel, who stood flabbergasted, afraid to say that once again he understood nothing.

"What about you?" Peter asked, point blank, in a suddenly sharp and cold tone of voice. "What do you want to be? Angel or beast?"

Daniel swallowed.

"I. . . I don't know."

MAGDALENA

She had been reading *Pinocchio* for a week.

Or rather, the first time she had read it, it had taken her only one day. Then she had reread it three more times, because she had waited for more directions on what to do from the stranger, but the sign had not changed. So she had spent half a day bored; besides eating, she had nothing to occupy the time.

She had enjoyed the book, although it bothered her to admit it. It was not a children's book or, at least, it was only in appearance. Even at the first, rapid reading, Magdalena had felt that there was something else behind the story, other meanings that she had not grasped, caught up as she was in the annoyance of having to read something that she already knew she might not like. But she had no other commitments, so she had reread it again, this time more slowly.

And then she read one more time, because she was sure she had missed something. By the end, she felt she knew it almost by heart and was not ashamed to confess that it was a really good story and that, once again, the stranger had been right.

On the eighth day since the book appeared, along with breakfast, another notebook popped up on the table, with a yellow cover this time. And next to that, a square mirror. The writing on the wall, however, had not changed. Magdalena understood that, as before, it was a suggestion. If she wanted, she could write. But what more did she need to write? She ate breakfast while looking out the window. The silence was broken only by the happy song of birds. She decided to go out, too, without the notebook, but with the mirror in her hand.

Since she had been there, she had not seen her own reflection. There were no combs, brushes, makeup, deodorant, or perfume. As a matter of fact, there was not even a toilet there, and Magdalena had not showered in a millennium! Maybe it was already a month? She didn't know exactly; talking about time, in that place, made no sense. And anyway, by now she was sending out a wild smell that she had even grown accustomed to. At home, she always wasted a lot of time getting ready before going out. In the woods, besides having nothing at hand to use for primping, there was no one who could appreciate it. Why waste energy on that?

Hesitantly, she finally looked at her reflection. She didn't recognize herself. Her face was rounder, but she did not feel the discomfort she would have imagined because, she felt, what had made it so was not simply the food, but the restful fact of finally feeling free. Free to be herself, because there was no one there who would judge her and, above all, because she had freed herself, thanks to the blue notebook, from the most implacable judge of all: old Magdalena.

She stared at the self that returned her gaze from the mirror for quite some time. Without makeup now, she paradoxically saw herself as more beautiful, more real. Her skin was fair and glowing, sprinkled with light freckles around her nose. She liked them and did not understand why, up to that point, she had hidden them under a layer of foundation. Her eyes were more honest, without that black outline cast around them.

Until that moment, leaving the house without makeup would have been like going out naked, revealing her fragility and vulnerability. Mascara and eye shadow had been her warrior armor, inside which the real Magdalena had taken refuge for so long. She realized that when she wore makeup she looked incredibly like Eliza — so much so that people often mistook them for sisters — and also like all the other girls she met at the usual club.

For a long time, perhaps most of my life, I was a wooden puppet maneuvered by others. I was never myself, neither when I was first in my class in junior high, nor when I was the bad girl who did everything she could to provoke and be different from her classmates. I wanted to be the best at everything: in school, in gymnastics. The model daughter, the model student, the model friend. But I felt that that wasn't really me, that there was a part of me that wanted to decide for itself without being accountable to anyone. It was a struggle to play that part every day. To be always smiling, always helpful. . . while sometimes I just wanted to cry and complain. But that's not like me, I told myself. After what happened with Marco, another Magdalena came out. I started wearing makeup, wearing black. . . I wanted to show others that I was strong, confident, determined, even though I wasn't at all. Things did not change; I still felt unhappy. In fact, maybe I was more so than before, because that wasn't me either. And then being delinquent all the time was even more tiring than playing the good girl. But I felt I had no alternative but to keep going that way. I didn't want to admit that I was wrong again. Besides, I didn't know

141

who I wanted to be or could be. In the end, I was
a puppet.

Now, however, I am here. I still don't know who
I am. I just know that I definitely want to be happy.
And I also know that before Marco, I was happy,
but maybe only because I was still very young and
I needed very little. A pair of new shoes, a chat
with mom, an evening at a pizza place with my
class, competition victory. Competitions — how
I miss gymnastics! When I was on the mat, mind
and body went together and there was no time
for unhappiness or bad thoughts. Gymnastics
made me feel happy and complete. And I gave it
up for that moron. Whoever put me here is prob-
ably a fool. I mean, I've been staying in a cabin in
the woods, alone, with no bathroom or phone, for
I don't know how long. Yet I think the stranger
knows what he's doing. Since I keep to myself, I
have a lot of time to think and maybe even figure
some things out. I don't want to be a puppet any-
more. I don't want to be wooden anymore. I want
to be myself, to figure out what I want and do it.

Magdalena got up from the table with her hand ach-
ing from all the writing. She felt her head heavy and
her heart light. She went outdoors again, stretched and
then bent forward until her fingers touched the tips of
her toes. She needed to move, to realign her soul with
her body. Although the boots were not the most comfortable shoe for it, she ran through the trees. It was
not like the first time she had done it, when she had
followed her instinct to flee, running off in a random
direction until her already depleted body was exhausted. Now she ran, filling her lungs with the good air and
her ears with the soothing sounds of the forest. When

she was out of breath, she slowed to a stop. Following a sudden impulse, she took off her shoes and socks and began to walk barefoot on the ground. It was cold and uneven, and the stones and bumps hurt her. Yet she found that pain pleasant. After much time spent walking, she returned, now perfectly relaxed, to the cabin. A great hamburger with fries was waiting for her on the table. Without the slightest hesitation she grabbed it, sinking her teeth into the soft bun. She swallowed the fries down in a few minutes and thought she would like more. For a moment, she felt a thrill run through her very much like happiness. As if somewhere in that place hid the answer she was looking for.

For a long time I felt wrong. I was like my parents wanted me to be, and I was no good. I was like Eliza and I was no good. Now I realize that, simply, I was different. I always knew inside that I was different. That I was going to do great things, even though I didn't know what. Then I made that giant mistake and my confidence was gone. I had done everything wrong; my life was ruined forever. Now, however, I am telling myself: you can make mistakes, everyone makes mistakes! The world does not stop if you make a mistake; life goes on and my happiness depends only on me. And my unhappiness also depends on me; there is no use blaming others. The first one to love me has to be me, and I want to start by not worrying all the time about what others may say about me. No one is as happy as they look, as they want to have others believe, in photos, in laughter. . . If only I knew what happiness means, what it is that I have to look for. . . Am I happy here? If being happy means learning to be alone, then maybe I'm starting to be happy. I don't have to have a boyfriend. I don't have to be first

143

in everything. Nor do I have to expect to be liked by everyone. I don't feel like going through all this effort anymore. So I'll just stay here. Maybe Pinocchio was happier in Toyland? And every time he was afraid to say no, so as not to look bad to others, it ended badly. I am like him; naive, stubborn, ungrateful. But if there is hope for a piece of wood, why couldn't there be for me? Yes, whatever, it's just a story. Yet it's not just a story. I also want to become flesh, I want to become a real person.

Once again, almost without realizing it, she had filled the entire notebook with her thoughts; they had come to her in an unstoppable flow, which stopped only when the pages were full. Writing helped clear her mind. And then, talking to herself, it seemed to her that she had a friend, that she was not alone — her own best friend. And true friends, she told herself, are the ones who tell you you're wrong when you're wrong, even if it means losing that friendship. She wanted to be honest from now on. She had done what she had done, been what she had been. But now, that strange adventure could turn into a new beginning. She smiled at herself in the mirror, winked one eye, and stuck out her tongue. Lightness and simplicity, these she longed for. With relief she also burned the yellow notebook, for she had now achieved the purpose for which it had been given to her. She fell asleep that night with a kind of excitement in her; what would the stranger's next move be?

When Magdalena awoke, she struggled for a moment to distinguish reality from a dream. She had dreamed that the stranger had entered the shack and put up a new sign in place of the old one. He had even stopped to stare at her, and she had seen his face clearly at last and told herself that she had not been mistaken; he was just beautiful. He had light eyes and a mysterious gaze.

Magdalena had not been able to decipher it. It was not sadness, it was not love. It was something else, but she lacked the right adjective to define it. One thing she did know, however: she would have done anything for him. Maybe it had not been just a dream. She turned toward the wall; the sign had indeed changed.

PLEASE SHEPHERD MY SHEEP.

She frowned uncomprehendingly. What was she to do? A bleating from the stable outside instantly removed all doubt from her mind.

The first to come toward her was a dog, a young Border Collie literally bursting with joy. Magdalena could not help but smile, infected by all that enthusiasm. From what little she knew about dogs, she could not explain how one who had never seen her before could give her so much cheer (instead of biting her in the calf). She also wondered how her unknown benefactor had managed to bring all those sheep into the stall in complete silence. Or perhaps, more likely, it was she who had slept as hard as she had ever done before.

Beside the little door, she noticed a stick taller than she was and a cloth bag hanging from a hook. She poked her head into the darkness of the room, through the upper doorway. The smell of the beasts was very intense, but strangely it did not bother her. The dog barked around her, jumping like a spring, its ears rising and falling with each leap. Magdalena crouched down to check the tag around his neck, "Shepard."

145

"So Shep, do you think we should go out?" she asked him as if she were talking to a person.

Almost as if he understood, the dog responded by barking. Magdalena opened the lower portion of the door and the dog came in, doing the devil's business. The sheep must have known him and were not frightened, but slowly began to come out of the stable. Magdalena slipped the bag over her shoulder and picked up the stick. With a few taps on her hip she held the sheep together. She marveled at the ease with which these gestures came to her. She looked at the dog, waiting for him to tell her where to go, and, indeed, he set off at a trot. The sheep went after him, and Magdalena closed the procession. She laughed, and she didn't even know why. She could see herself from the outside with the shepherd's bag and staff and found it completely strange, yet natural. She watched the huge butts of the sheep advancing in front of her, swaying and lurching, and it seemed like the funniest situation. Every so often one would turn and stare at her as if to verify that there was someone who knew where they were going. Instead, she had no idea and relied on a crazy dog.

When Shepard decided they had arrived at the right place, Magdalena looked around. Suddenly the forest had opened into a wide green clearing. Her gaze was momentarily disoriented by the total lack of trees. There was only a large stone in the middle of the meadow, and Magdalena went to sit on it. The sun warmed her and the contact with the rock was pleasant.

The morning passed in this way: Magdalena sat on the rock and kept watch so that the sheep never strayed too far — though it was then Shepard who would run to retrieve them if they started to leave, barking like a madman. When she began to get bored, to kill time she set about naming each animal. She took a long time, looking for the details that made one sheep recognizable from the other. The one that bothered all the others and did nothing but petulant bleating she named Raspa, after her obnoxious math teacher. That little revenge gave her satisfaction. The tiniest one, whose best grass was stolen by the others without uttering a bleat, she called Maddy, as she was called in junior high school. But at a certain point she no longer wanted anyone to call her that. If they had to use a nickname, she preferred Mad, like "crazy," because by then she felt really out of her mind.

When she got hungry, she stuck her hand into the bag and found bread and cheese, a handful of olives and an apple. Nothing out of the ordinary, but the crisp air of the place had put such an appetite in her that it felt like the best meal ever. She returned to homebase when it seemed to her that the sky was getting too dark. The sheep returned meekly to the stable, and Magdalena, followed by Shep, returned to the shack.

Standing in the doorway, she gasped like a child who had caught Santa Claus in the act: red as a rose, on the table, shone a magnificent ribbon, the kind Magdalena used when she was still doing rhythmic gymnastics. She felt a pang in her heart, as if the stranger had left her a real declaration of love on the coffee table. That tape reminded her of Marco, of course. Yet it also called to her mind an almost intolerable feeling of happiness. She felt the passion for the ribbon flowing back into her like a river that has broken its banks. She touched it with her fingers, almost fearfully, as if it were something precious. Then she grabbed it firmly and stepped out into the open. With a familiar gesture she unfurled it, releasing waves and circles in the air. She remembered the steps of the exercise she had presented at the last competition. Forgetting where she was, as if she were on the gym mat, she began to bend, jump, roll. . . But her shoes were not the best, the ground was hard, and her arms and legs no longer responded as they should. She had lost elasticity and there was not enough room there; the tape was constantly getting stuck in branches and bushes. She tried a throw and missed the catch. She tried and tried again, but she needed practice. There was little light now, and this did not allow her to judge distances well, or so she justified herself, lest she admit she was no longer capable. Out of breath and with sweat freezing on her back, she re-entered the shack.

She was covered with dust and dirt and her hair was full of leaves and twigs. She had skinned her knee and scratched her neck, probably on a stone. As she dried herself in front of the stove, her body felt the wounds and bruises it had taken, which, earlier, intoxicated by holding a ribbon in her hands again, she had not even noticed. She watched as she rewound it; it had gotten dirty and lost much of its beauty. Without knowing why, Magdalena began to cry. A strange emotion of sadness and happiness together had assailed her. Shep came to lick her face. "You have terrible breath, Shep," she observed, lending herself to that saliva bath, then she burst out laughing through her tears. She must have looked awful, she told herself, but she also felt wonderful. The boiling water on the stove, mixed with the cold water, allowed her to wash herself, but not as she would have liked. She sighed; she definitely needed a shower. She could still smell the stench of sheep on her. She put on her clean clothes, nothing more than an old jumpsuit she had found on the bed, and literally devoured the cold pasta with beans that the stranger had left on the table for her, along with the tape. She felt that this man, she did not know how, knew everything about her, even what she needed before she realized it herself. Even Shep is indispensable, she told herself as she watched him amusedly, meticulously cleaning the plate with his very long, pink tongue. She really needed company, even if it was that of a dog. Of the stranger, she now remembered his face only vaguely but, in a way that only a girl of 16 can know, she was sure she loved him.

She fell asleep on the bed thinking of him, smiling as she watched sleeping Shep on the floor, moving his paws, dreaming of running on the lawn again. *Perhaps*, thought Magdalena, *I should follow his lead* – pure joy and lightness.

It now seemed to Magdalena that she was living outside of time, in an eternal present, with almost no past and no need to think necessarily about any future. What had been was full of pain. What was not yet was frightening, for all the pain it still concealed. The now was serene and relaxed, with no obligations or duties. There were no roles to play. Magdalena did not have to prove anything to anyone, and someone cared for her, making her feel safe and loved. Every morning, she slipped into her work clothes, marveled at Shep's undiminished joy and let it rub off on her, opened the stable door and led the sheep out to pasture. She would spend the day outside, carry the tape and perform the exercises humming the music with which she had rehearsed far too long ago. She would take off her shoes. The grass was better than hard earth for jumping; she would tie her hair in a tight bun and begin to warm up her muscles. Then she would wave to an invisible jury and close her eyes for a moment to concentrate. As soon as the music began to play in her head, she would raise her head sharply with the air of someone who knows what she is doing. Then, when she began to draw figures in the air with the tape, Shep would literally go crazy and start barking and circling around her as if to bite her, causing her to stumble. But she did not lose concentration and continued with the exercise, increasing the difficulty each time, never giving up when she made a mistake, trying and trying again until everything was perfect. Gymnastics required sacrifice and determination, but she was not afraid. After a week of practice, she began to feel more confident; she had already regained some agility. She hardly missed her grip and was snappy and fast again. But there was still a lot of catching up to do. Her companions had to be far ahead of her by now. The important thing, however, was that she was finally, after a long time, feeling good.

One night, she was awakened by dull banging coming from the barn. Shep jumped up, barking at the door. Magdalena, seeing almost nothing in the darkness, came out with her heart pounding. She shivered from the cold and from a sudden cry that rose from the thicket of branches. It sounded like a woman's scream. It must be a bird of some kind, she reassured herself as she saw that Shep took no notice of it. Tugging to pull on her jacket, she quickened her pace to keep up with him and not be alone out there. In the stable, Snowball walked around in the space available, bleating, bumping against the other sheep. There was little light, just that of the moonlight filtering through the door.

"Calm down," she said, speaking mostly to herself.

She tried to stop it as it passed her, but it slipped through her hands, surprisingly nimble. There was something odd about her backside.

"Oh dear!" Magdalena felt sick.

Inside, she knew it would happen sooner or later. She had noticed that Snowball had gotten very swollen recently. That thing sticking out of her backside must have been the muzzle of her little lamb. What was she to do? She shuddered, this time in revulsion. For nothing in the world would she touch Snowball or the lamb. It was one thing to shepherd sheep and quite another to take part in that scary scene, without even having a clue where to put her hands. She exited the stable suppressing a gasp. Then she breathed deeply, trying futilely to purge from her memory what she had just seen.

"Help!" she cried, hoping the stranger could hear her, but her voice, bouncing from tree trunk to tree trunk, startled her.

Who was she asking for help from? Imagine if he didn't know what was happening! He simply wanted her to manage on her own. In a sense of desperate powerlessness, she turned to Shep, who had followed her outside, saying, "Do you know what should be done?"

Shep, probably the most intelligent beast in the known universe, ran in and chased Snowball; then he stood in front of her barking. Snowball threw herself to the floor, as if obeying an order. The dog then turned to Magdalena. Now it was her turn.

"But what should I do?" she asked, despairingly.

Shep sniffed the lamb's snout, licked it, and then looked up at Magdalena. A small piece of slimy face and hoof and a few inches of fore shank could be seen.

"Okay, okay!" snapped Magdalena, turning to Shep. "Oh my God," she said to herself, "I can't believe I'm really doing this!"

Overcoming her revulsion, she touched the paw, but retracted her hand with a gasp. The stuff covering it looked like egg white, but was of a thicker, more elastic consistency.

"No, I can't do it. . ." whimpered Magdalena in panic.

Shep walked halfway around her and sat down, staring at her encouragingly and confidently.

"Hownastyhownastyhownasty."

With her eyes closed, she began to pull on the paw.

Then, all at once, the little lamb was out. Magdalena cautiously opened one eye; she was not sure she wanted to see. But Snowball was already on her feet. She had gulped down the placenta and was now licking her baby. It was motionless and appeared to be dead. Then, perhaps from the tickling of his mother's tongue, he quivered all over from his ears to his tail. His mother was licking him thoroughly, on all sides. Magdalena stood watching the scene. By the end of the "bath," the lamb's coat was white and curly. And even before she herself had recovered, the lamb tried to stand on its own hooves. Without quite understanding why, Magdalena burst into tears. It had been unbelievably gross, yet she sensed a nameless beauty behind all that had

152

happened. She took the baby in her arms; it was moist and warm, the most fragile thing she had ever held.

She re-entered the shed, rinsed off the remnants of childbirth and threw herself on the bed, exhausted.

After that unique night in which she went through trial by fire, Magdalena assisted in the birth of two more sheep. The amazing thing was that the nastiness completely disappeared and only wonder remained. She felt something inexpressible inside, a kind of urge to weep that quivered like a leaf attached to its slender branch, tormented by the wind. It was an entanglement of thoughts, a yearning that would erupt at any moment.

I will stay here forever, thought Magdalena one night, after seeing a new little lamb being born. But, the next morning, the paper had changed.

THANK YOU FOR WHAT YOU HAVE DONE.
YOUR TIME HERE IS COMPLETED.

She turned the paper over and there was a map.

ELIJAH

He could no longer remember who he was, not even his own name, if he ever had one, much less how he had ended up there, what he was doing there, and how long he had been there. Somewhere in him there was still a glimmer of reason, but mostly he moved by instinct. The smells, the noises. . . He was able to smell danger, if there was any nearby, like the night that strange being had approached him, perhaps an animal. Elijah had never seen anything like it. It was big and shaggy. It had snarled at him and bared its fangs, but he had put it to flight with a fierce scream. There were images, in his head, that followed one another as in an unconnected and meaningless dream. There was another place, different from the one he was in now, with dazzling lights and the sound of drums, and a white man who had tricked him. When he thought of him, a red haze descended into his eyes and his jaw clenched until it creaked. He wanted to kill him; he did not know why. There was also another man, who looked like him, telling him things he could not remember. A woman who was crying. A blond female who made the hair on his head stand up in excitement if he only thought of her. He couldn't remember her name, but he knew he wanted her. Then there was that cursed forest. Somewhere there he had met another like him. They had fought, this he remembered, then he had left. And since then he had been wandering around looking for a way out, but there was clearly no way out. It shouldn't be hard to get out of a forest, he had thought at first; just follow the same direction forward, on and on. It had to end somewhere. Yet it had not worked, and he had probably been going in circles. Now his mind could no longer reason. He was just hungry, so hungry, and a fierce anger consumed him from within and clouded his mind.

He reached the bank of a river. He drank great mouthfuls. He jerked up. There was a man under the water – his hair was standing on end, and he was staring at him with evil eyes. Elijah anticipated his move and struck him with his hand. The fist sank into the water and the man disappeared. He got to his feet again, checking to make sure he did not return. When the waters had calmed down, there he was again, just under the water, dirty and covered in rags, looking at him with a smile that he did not like at all. Elijah picked up a large stone and threw it into the water; the stranger disappeared again. The rock must have caught him, he told himself, and he walked away from the river, satisfied. He was hungry now. A bird perched not far from him. Like a cat, he was on top of it, grabbed it with his hands, and bit it on the neck. Warm blood trickled down his body, and the smell made Elijah's nostrils flare. The woods had made him as stealthy and silent as an Indian; anger had done the rest. He threw what was left of the bird to the ground and walked away, sniffing the air, searching with his eyes for something else to devour. He climbed the trunk of a tree, scouring it branch by branch, looking for a nest. There must have been one nearby, because a large black-and-white bird swooped down on him to prevent him from moving upward. Elijah instinctively shielded his eyes with his hands, loosened his grip, and slipped, screaming in anger. He fell to the ground, landing badly on his feet. The nail of one hand had been torn off, and a bulge in the trunk had injured his foot. He stood staring at himself for a while. He remembered that he, at one time, had shoes. He must have taken them off, but he could not remember when or where. He crouched on the ground and, squirming all over, licked the blood from his wound.

A rustling behind him startled him. He spotted a hare moving through the bushes. He sprang like a panther and set off in pursuit, feeling no more pain. The hare scrambled left and right, but Elijah kept up with it, anticipating its every move. He could feel its fear in his nostrils and under his skin, and this gave him strength. He saw not far away the entrance to the den, hidden among the roots of a tree. He pushed up on his legs and sprinted, grabbing the hare an instant before it slipped inside to safety. He held her tightly by the ears as the hare struggled desperately. He looked into its round eyes, muzzle to muzzle, and read terror in them. He smiled. With a lightning snap he slammed the animal against the trunk of the tree, and it went limp in his hands. He bit it on the neck, spitting out a tuft of hair on the ground; he slipped his fingers into the hole that had formed on the fur and expanded it. He tore away the skin, which made a dull, ragged noise. At last, he had his meal.

PART THREE

GABRIEL

"Gabriel, I know very well that you know the answer. Go ahead and speak."

With divine patience, Mrs. Speranza stared at the boy in front of her, who was locked in impenetrable silence. Gabriel could not stand that calm, confident look, those round owl eyes. He felt anger coming on bitterly, like indigestion.

"Gabriel, will you explain to me why you don't want to answer?"

The silence weighed on everyone like a dead body and to most seemed intolerable, but not to her. "I know how you feel," she said, "but. . ."

It's too much! thought Gabriel, who at that point exploded. First speaking through his teeth, then raising his voice higher and higher.

"She doesn't know a damn thing. No one can know how I feel."

He leapt to his feet and clung to the desk, causing it to shake. A nearby classmate ducked instinctively, and those in the classroom feared they would see it fly over the teacher's head any second. They were frozen in shock.

"And I don't answer her questions, because this stuff is useless. It's all bullshit and she's a loser, even if no one has ever told her!"

He went out, slamming the door. All eyes focused on the teacher, who, with enviable self-control, was staring at an undefined spot on the back wall of the classroom. Jacob raised a hand.

"Yes?" asked the teacher, as if awakening.

"In my opinion, you have to write him a disciplinary note; you can't let him insult you like that."

Ever since Gabriel had been ostracized by his nervous breakdown, Jacob had been aspiring for the coveted top spot in the class.

"I'm not insulted at all," replied the teacher seriously.

She didn't look flustered but Jenny, who was watching the scene from the first desk, was convinced that the teacher was intimately more bothered by Jacob's lousy careerism than by Gabriel's ugly words.

Professor Speranza flipped through the register; in the past month Gabriel had been skipping class a lot. The few times he had gone to school, he had gotten at least two notes a day. For years, he had been the best in the class, and now he had collapsed. It was utterly pointless to rage; disciplinary measures with him were useless.

"Mrs. Speranza . . ." Jenny had raised her hand.

"Yes, Jenny, what is it?"

"Gabriel is having a hard time since his brother died. . ."

She was interrupted just then by Gabriel bursting back into the classroom, which in fact he did in time to hear the last part of the sentence. He looked at Jenny with murderous hatred.

"Shut up, Nightmare, I don't need your defense."

"Gabriel!"

At that point, the teacher became visibly upset. Jenny stood mute; her eyes downcast. From where he stood, Gabriel could not see her lips trembling, as she was on the verge of tears.

"Listen to me well, Gabriel: if you offend me, I don't care. I am above your words and they don't touch me. But I can't let it go when you insult a friend of yours."

In response, Gabriel grabbed his backpack and walked out of the classroom again, slamming the door. Twenty-five pairs of eyes went to the teacher again, who, this time, with a firm hand but without giving any sign of anger or agitation, wrote yet another note in the register. It was of no use, she was aware, and, to be honest, more than anything else she was distressed by the idea of having to call Gabriel's home to inform his parents of the situation. It was like attacking the Red Cross.

"Mrs. Speranza. . ." the voice of Jenny rose again, dimly. "I don't care what he said. I'm not offended. I know he's sick. Don't put another note on his record."

Her teacher smiled sadly at her. Jenny had been the most beautiful girl in high school until a bad fire accident disfigured her. The red-and-white scar, veined like wrinkled plastic, stretched from behind her ear to below her neck, rising then to lap one cheek. Still, Jenny continued to be beautiful in the teacher's eyes —- perhaps even more beautiful than before. She knew the boys did not think so; their idea of perfection did not include strange abnormalities of the epidermis. As proof of this, since the accident, Jenny had not had any more boyfriends. That's why it was horrible what Gabriel had said to her; he had really crossed the line.

"Don't worry, Jenny. Thank you. Let's resume the lesson."

Heads lowered back to their books, and for the next hour the teacher's quiet voice bounced between the four walls of the classroom, otherwise silent as if it was empty.

Gabriel spent a lot of time walking around the downtown area, pacing like a madman. He was noisily blowing air through his nose, like a bull ready to charge, to let out all the anger that was choking him.

"Hey, Michael!" a voice called to him.

He knew him by sight; it was Brandon, a friend of his brother's.

"They told me you were dead! What an idiotic joke, and I had believed it. I even cried!"

"Yeah, but here I am," Gabriel gave a half-smile. He had no desire to contradict him or to explain. "Sorry, but I really have to go," he cut it short.

"Sure!" said the other, giving him a slap on the shoulder, "See you around!"

Gabriel quickened his pace to put as much distance as possible between him and Brandon. His gaze fell on a shop window, in which he saw his reflection. Since Michael had died, he had not cut his hair. It was understandable that Brandon had taken him for Michael; if he kept his hair that way, they were practically identical. As a child, he hated being mistaken for his brother; often not even Dad could tell the twins apart. Mom did, however. Always. She said Gabriel had his own way of tilting his head, more shy, less confident than Michael. *A detail invisible to everyone but my mother,* thought Gabriel, who had not realized that this attitude made him so recognizable in her eyes. However, it was true: of the two, he was the more docile one. Michael had always been the rebel, the oppositional one, the anti-everything. He had been driving his parents crazy since kindergarten, getting into one mischief after another. The last one, however, had proven to be irreversible.

That had been the last time he had made Mom cry. Gabriel had hated him, for all the harm he did to her. They had come to blows many times, and Michael almost always won, but only because Gabriel did not really want to hurt him. But then Gabriel had joined the gym, boxing, and no one had believed, then, that it was the right sport for him. But he had taken to it. The trainer called him "The Iceman" because he hit hard but never lost control. With boxing, he was rational, systematic; that's why he was strong, because he always stayed sharp. Until Michael died.

What a sleazy way to go. Alone, drunk, and stoned. At least that was what the police, who had found him in the club's bathroom, had said. The autopsy confirmed this, because no witnesses to the fact had been found.

One could never be the same after seeing what Gabriel had seen: his brother dead, deep-frozen on top of a metal plate. He had had to go to the morgue, because he would not let Mom in alone with Dad. Dad would not have had the right words, assuming there were any. In fact, he had just stood there, his face as expressionless as ever, inscrutable. A statue. Gabriel, on the other hand, had hugged his mother and tried to be strong for both of them. But Michael — why had it ended like that? His corpse lay there, pale, with blue veins, running all over, showing under his skin. His hair was slicked back in a way he would never have worn it. It must have been the doctors who had done the autopsy, or the nurses who had cleaned him up afterwards, who had combed it like that. This sight of Michael was worse than any horror movie he had ever seen, and it came back to him again and again.

No, one could never be the same after seeing what he had seen. In his nightmares he saw that it was he, Gabriel, lying dead on that steel bed. He was looking at his own cadaver. Michael, in leaving this world, had taken away an important piece of him.

If he had hated Michael for all the harm he had done to Mom, why was he now the one to make her suffer? He didn't want to, yet for the moment he was unable to do anything else. He was making a mess at school. He had quit even his long-standing group of friends. He despised being looked at with pity; he didn't want anyone's pity. He wanted to be alone, to think, even if he couldn't. His brain was off, in blackout mode.

Some days, he wanted to die, too. He didn't even care about Veronica, whom he had earlier believed to be the love of his life. He had jilted her without a tear, while she had screeched and pleaded and then threatened to kill herself. But he had not given in. He simply no longer felt anything — nothing for her, nothing for anyone, not even for himself. Then Veronica had recovered, and when she heard about the mess Gabriel was making at school, she felt almost lucky to have escaped it. In fact, she had taken up with someone else right away, a lanky college guy, with a car. Even then Gabriel had felt nothing; not even a reaction to the news. He thought only of Michael, of the thousand things they had done together, of their understanding of each other without speaking, just with a single glance. Even when they didn't get along, argued, or hit each other, it had been beautiful to have a twin brother. It had been beautiful. Now it was a nightmare.

Gabriel was certain that he was on the verge of going insane. He spent his mornings in the gym, punching anyone who would lend themselves to training with him. Occasionally, he would go to school, he couldn't even say why. Sometimes he spent the night walking around downtown.

Like that night.

"Hi Michael!" It was the annoying voice of Brandon again. But there was someone with him that Gabriel did not know, and he gave Brandon an elbow between the ribs.

"It's not Michael, you idiot! It's his brother," he heard him hiss. "I told you, Michael is dead!"

Brandon turned red and put on a foolish expression.

"It's not a problem," Gabriel said; of the three, he was the one who wanted to end that conversation first.

Brandon scratched his head with a dumbfounded expression and walked away.

"Hey, I'm sorry about your brother," quipped the unknown guy.

"Yes, everyone is sorry," replied Gabriel, using a matter-of-fact phrase.

"I'm Anthony," he said, holding out his hand. "I was Michael's best friend."

He had a powerful grip. Gabriel got a good look at his face; he seemed like a nice guy. A minute before, he didn't even know he existed. Michael had never mentioned him. But then again, they had stopped hanging out for years; Gabriel didn't like the guys Michael had started associating with, people with few boundaries. He had almost gone crazy trying to reason with him, but Michael won on that score, too.

"Your life is your own!" he had yelled in his face, earning himself a punch in the mouth, immediately followed by another on the eyebrow. "Have it your way!" Gabriel added, exasperated by the taste of blood in his mouth and half-blinded by what was coming down his eyebrow. "Drop dead!"

And Michael in turn had taken him at his word and dropped dead. A month later.

That memory filled him with anguish; those were the last words they had exchanged. There had been no time to clarify, to apologize. The news that Michael had died had burst like a bomb in their house at five in the morning. After that day, every time the phone rang, at any hour, his heart jumped into his throat and Gabriel struggled to regain control of himself.

"Want a beer?" asked Anthony, bringing him back to reality.

They each took a can and sat down on the steps of a closed church to drink. Gabriel had no desire to be there and would not have been able to say why he had stayed. There was something inside him, like a feeling of foreboding, that kept him glued to those dirty steps. He had the feeling that something important was about to happen, although he could not imagine what. Anthony pulled out a joint and started smoking; he seemed tense and his hand was shaking. After a few puffs, he began to babble, now more relaxed; disconnected words came flowing out of his mouth. He had the look of someone who needed to clear his conscience. He mumbled without looking at Gabriel's face, as if ashamed of something, speaking more to himself than anyone else.

"Hey, yeah . . . I mean . . . I'm really sorry about your brother; he was a good guy," he exclaimed.

"No, he wasn't quite," commented Gabriel, staring into space.

He hated and loved Michael at the same time, and wished he could have him alive there, just to punch him, to bury him with slaps and insults.

"I just wanted to tell you that it wasn't my fault that night," Anthony continued in a voice as whiny as a child's.

Gabriel pricked up his ears. "Were you there?" he quickly asked, aiming his gaze straight at him.

"Yes," Anthony admitted. "I told him to let it go, but he didn't listen to me."

"How did it happen? Who killed him? Why didn't you tell the police?" snapped Gabriel immediately, throwing at him all the questions he had been chewing on since the morning of the phone call.

"I don't know anything," he stiffened immediately, hearing the police mentioned. But Gabriel could tell that he knew more than he was letting on.

"You have to tell me, Anthony. You have to tell me for Michael, too, who died alone like a dog in that bathroom!"

Gabriel was beside himself and he felt like he was going to have an accident. The autopsy had been clear; his brother had died of a heart attack from an overdose. It had taken two months for these medical conclusions to be reached, and the people who did not want to be involved had meanwhile slipped away. The investigation was still ongoing, of course, but he, in his house, seemed to be the only one who still wanted to know. "What's the point?" his grief-stricken mother asked him. "'Michael is gone."

"Just to catch the bastards who sold him that stuff, and to make them stop killing people!" shouted Gabriel every time she responded like this.

It was true and they both knew it, but Michael was not "people," he was her son, Gabriel told himself; the pain prevented his mother from reasoning. In addition, his father had not said a word since the night of the phone call, keeping it all inside. Gabriel would have preferred for him to freak out or scream rather than show that robotic self-control. But his father was like that, and with his mother he had stopped talking about the incident early on, because she did not want to continually reopen the wound. He had met Anthony now, though, and it couldn't have been by accident. Now he will know what had happened that night.

Anthony hesitated. Gabriel could tell that he wanted to talk and at the same time his fear of something was holding him back.

"Come on, damn it!" Gabriel lost his temper. "You have to tell me!" he shouted, grabbing him by the jacket and shaking him.

Anthony lowered his gaze and did not flinch; Gabriel realized he was cracking.

"There was stuff involved — a heroin deal."

Heroin, yes; the doctors had said so.

"They owed him money, your brother, for a job he did."

"What job? Who owed him money?" Gabriel's mouth had gone dry.

"Look, I don't really know anything about it," Anthony backed away, already regretting having said too much.

"Yes, you do! If you were really his best friend, tell me now."

Anthony swallowed as if he had a tennis ball in his throat, then continued. "Michael had been selling stuff for them. . ."

Was his brother a drug dealer? Gabriel felt his strength fail him; he let go of Anthony's jacket, which he was still clutching between his fingers, and lowered his head. What a disappointment. What a huge disappointment. He knew that Michael smoked, but he believed that heroin had been a one-time fatal mistake. He hadn't realized that he had gone so far, that he'd gotten into such a mess.

"And then what?" he asked almost voicelessly.

"And they paid him with that stuff. It was his first time doing heroin. . ." Anthony whimpered. "He offered it to me, too, but I refused it that night." He wiped his nose with a sleeve. He began to sob, out of guilt and the knowledge that he had gotten away unscathed.

Gabriel was stunned by the discovery, but he managed to regain his speech. "Do you remember those people? Where can I find them?"

Anthony looked him straight in the face, startled. Gabriel felt his throat close up, waiting for the answer. He encouraged him with a nod.

"They changed clubs," he said. "But it's better not to have anything to do with them, take it from me."

It took all his insistence to get the name of the new club, and finally Anthony spit it out. "Don't go there," he insisted, trying to warn him. "Those guys are capable of anything." He didn't want that on his conscience as well.

"Don't worry," Gabriel reassured him. He didn't know what he wanted to do either.

Gabriel thought and thought about it for days. Michael was dead. What was the point of continuing down this road? Yet he wanted to look into the faces of those who had last seen his brother alive. He was killed by his own hands, but they had given him the stuff. He just wanted to talk to them, explain to them what they had done to him and his family. He wanted to tell them what kind of guy Michael was, list all the things they could never live together again. Over and over, he would rehearse in his head the speech he wanted to make, word for word. It didn't really matter anyway; he would never decide to go to that club.

Months had passed since Michael had died, and with each passing day Gabriel was getting worse. Then one evening he felt that the time had come. It was Friday; not just another day, but their birthday, his and Michael's, only Michael wouldn't be there. They would have turned 18; they had talked for a long time about their 18th birthday party, about invitations, and they had even argued, because their friends were too different. Yet they would never give up celebrating together. Everyone in the family remembered this, clearly. That morning, while having breakfast, his mother had wished him happy birthday and, kissing him on the head, she had stood behind him, holding him close. Gabriel knew perfectly well what she was thinking. It was on everyone's mind. An obsession for him. The void left by Michael cried out; his empty chair cried out, the deserted room, the corridors devoid of his loud laughter, his cheerful, unruly voice. Gabriel had to honor his brother's memory. He was dealing and had died of an overdose, okay, but he could have had the rest of his life to realize his mistakes and change his ways, if only they had given him the chance.

"Michael," he said to himself in the mirror before leaving the house, "give me a hand."

It was late and there were a lot of people at the club. Anthony had finally worked up the courage to accompany him, more than anything else, probably, to make sure he didn't do something stupid. He had the face of someone who would rather be anywhere than there. "Those are the guys over there," Anthony pointed, trying to blend in as he was terrified of the possibility of being noticed. "Forget it," he begged him, unintentionally repeating the last words he had said to Michael on the night of his death.

Don't go, advised a dim voice inside him. Gabriel watched them. They were neatly dressed; he had expected different types. Maybe a little disheveled, as his brother was, not mommy's boys. They were laughing boisterously with the air of being the bosses of the place. *How could anyone laugh like that,* thought Gabriel, *knowing they had killed a person?* The news had appeared in all the papers; it was impossible for them to ignore it. Or maybe, even, they were there when Michael's body had been found in the bathroom. The fact that they had changed clubs proved that they were aware of what had happened. So there it was, the truth: they couldn't have cared less. Gabriel felt a great anger mounting inside. He took a deep breath and pushed straight toward the pack. When he appeared in their midst, they all fell silent; some visibly whitened. Gabriel knew perfectly well what had happened: they thought they were looking at a dead man.

"Do you recognize me?" he asked seriously and confidently, increasing their fear.

They all took a step back, except for one, who did not flinch an inch. He was the best dressed one, and from the way his friends looked at him it was clear that he must be the leader. Gabriel could not figure out his age, but the watch he sported on his wrist must have been worth a thousand dollars. Flaunting a jaded air, he cast a glance at the watch. "Come on, guys, I have an appointment."

He made to leave, ignoring Gabriel as if he were invisible.

"We need to talk first."

"I don't even know who you are. Or rather, I know you're not who you seem," he said arrogantly, understanding the situation on the fly. "You're his brother, aren't you?"

He doesn't have the courage to mention Michael, thought Gabriel with his breathing coming in short, agitated breaths.

"Do you know how he died?" Gabriel asked him point-blank, wasting no time. He wanted to see if he had the courage to tell the truth, to take responsibility and admit that he was the one who gave him the stuff that killed him.

"No," he said, staring shamelessly into his eyes, as if to challenge him.

Everything happened too quickly. The guy could not have known that Gabriel was a boxer, and that he would never have expected that someone a half-foot shorter than he was would have thrown such a punch. The blow exploded from Gabriel instinctively, without allowing him to measure its force. The uppercut threw back his opponent, who lost his balance and fell, hitting his head on the counter. Gabriel watched him sag like a puppet of sawdust and remain motionless on the ground.

His friends in the pack rushed to help.

"Matthew!" they called to him, but the man showed no signs of life.

Someone shouted for an ambulance. Gabriel, motionless and mute, watched the scene. The boy was on the ground and not regaining consciousness. A glass of ice water with ice cubes still in it had been thrown in his face, but the boy was not opening his eyes.

"Is he breathing?" someone asked.

"How long does the ambulance take?" cried a girl, perhaps his girlfriend, sobbing.

"Who did this?" asked another.

Things had happened so fast, few had seen.

"He did it!" shouted one of the pack kneeling on the ground, pointing at Gabriel with one finger. "He said he was going to kill him."

"It's true! I heard it too!" added another.

"Don't let him out!" shouted someone from the door.

But Gabriel was completely unable to move. What had he done? It had only been a punch. He had given and taken many in the ring. Instead, Matthew had gone down like a dummy. What now? Oh God, what now? His mind couldn't think.

The ambulance arrived along with the police, whom someone else must have called. Without resistance, absent as if he were in someone else's body, Gabriel allowed himself to be arrested. The ambulance workers had surrounded Matthew, and Gabriel wished he knew what was going on. He wanted to hear them say that he was alive, that everything was all right. The cops didn't give him the time to find out. They grabbed him under the armpits, lifting him practically out of the way, and loaded him into the squad car.

They took him to police headquarters. Gabriel, inebriated, could not even give general answers. They searched him and found his ID in his pocket.

"Do you remember what happened?" a man's voice asked him gently. It must have been the commissioner.

It seemed to Gabriel that he could no longer speak. His brain was completely disconnected. Had he been arrested? How was Matthew doing? He looked at his hands, lying dormant on his legs, unable to believe that they could have hurt someone so much.

"Ah," commented the commissioner seriously, reading his ID card, "18 years old just today! Happy birthday. And welcome to the world of 18."

Gabriel raised his face and looked for the first time at the man in front of him. His words rang in his head. He could not tell if there was irony in them or just deep sadness.

They remained staring at each other like that for a while, without saying anything else.

The first night in the cell had been the worst. He still had not heard anything about Matthew, he did not understand why he was there, and he did not know how long he would stay there. Above all, he was nagged by the thought of his parents. Had they been informed? And if they had, what did they think of him now? Perhaps they would stop considering him their son. Maybe they would never want to see him again. He had gone to that club to resolve the situation, to get the answers he was looking for, but instead he had made an even bigger mess. He cried all night. He sat on the cold floor, with his head between his knees and his hands pressed over his ears, but he still couldn't keep those thoughts from coming to him. He hoped not to wake up the next morning, not to see the new day, as black as the night and as those to come.

The days that followed were convulsive and confusing. Newspapers headlined ruthlessly and his name was everywhere. "The Mommy's Son Murderer," they called him. They had already delivered their verdict, even before Gabriel set foot in court, and he would have wanted to defend himself, to say he was not a murderer, that it was an accident, but who would believe him? Matthew, he had been told, had died a few hours after he arrived at the hospital.

His father hired a lawyer friend. It was he who had given Gabriel the news of Matthew's death and explained to him how things were. He seemed to be a kind and knowledgeable person and asked him precise, circumstantial questions. He did not reassure him one bit, he did not give him false hope. Gabriel would have liked him to lie, to tell him that everything would be all right.

Instead, the lawyer did not mince words, "I understand your situation," he said, but he weighed every word.

"So you started it," the lawyer asked him.

"Yes," Gabriel admitted, never able to lie.

"And you went there on purpose."

"Yes," he replied again. "I knew those people there gave the heroin to Michael," he tried to defend himself. "But I didn't go with the intention of beating anyone up. I just wanted to talk to those guys. They provoked me. I didn't expect that with one punch. . ." he was unable to finish the sentence. He could not say that he had killed a person.

"You are a boxer, Gabriel. And you were not in the ring."

He remained silent; he knew the lawyer was right. He knew where to strike to hurt. And a part of him told him that he deserved prison, since because of him a person had died. Even though it happened also because he'd had some damn bad luck, that fact didn't change things. Somewhere, a phone had rung in the night, and now there was a mother mourning her son, as his own mother had mourned for Michael. And he was the cause of all that pain. He asked the lawyer if he had seen his parents. He had not asked to meet them; he was afraid of his father's eyes and his mother's tears. He had never let them down in his life. He had always been a perfect son, and all at once he had hurt them more than Michael had ever hurt them. He told himself that it was better to have a dead son and be pitied than one who was alive but in prison, a public shame to his parents.

The first meeting with his mother was heart-breaking. Gabriel did not have the courage to look her in the face. He did not know whether he would see reproach, sorrow, anger, or who knows what else in it. At first, he remained seated, head bowed. He did not want to cry. He felt full of shame and guilt. His mother said nothing, but Gabriel sensed her eyes on him. Then she walked over and hugged him. "Be brave."

Her voice did not tremble; it was sweet and all her love for him could be heard in it. He did not expect this and burst into sobs. She didn't tell him not to cry; she just held him even tighter, like when he was a baby and he hurt himself, or when Michael was picking on him, or when he had screwed up somehow.

"Sorry," he managed to say. "Sorry," he repeated, and he could have gone on and on, with all the guilt eating away at him from within. "I swear I didn't mean to!"

"I know. I know who you are. We will not leave you alone, me and Dad. Let's just see what happens, okay?" She brushed the hair out of his face.

At the mention of his father's name, Gabriel felt sick.

"What does Dad say?"

"What do you want him to say. . .?"

"Is he ashamed of me?" It was the thing that distressed him most.

"No, Gabriel. He knows it was an accident. Besides, you know him; he has never cared about what other people think. Nor has he been listening to them this time. He doesn't read the newspapers and he doesn't watch TV."

"Why didn't he come, then?"

His mother sighed. "He thought he couldn't stand it, seeing you here," she said, lowering her eyes to the floor.

Gabriel thought back to his father, completely dumbfounded in the morgue. He realized once again that, of his parents, the weaker one was not his mother. His father kept everything inside, and was so cold that he seemed to be feeling nothing, and this pushed everyone away. Yet that detachment was just an act in the end.

"Listen to me, Gabriel." His mother took his face in her hands. "We will face everything together. The trial, the sentencing, the appeal if we have to. You just promise me that you won't get discouraged, okay?"

Gabriel nodded, starting to cry again.

The first weeks in jail were a nightmare. Gabriel spent them in absolute silence. He did not eat or sleep. His head worked day and night. As soon as he closed his eyes, he saw Matthew going down like a puppet and his friend's finger pointed at him; he heard the screams, the stomping of the feet of those around him, the sirens of the ambulance. His conscience gave him no peace. He had killed a person. He thought back to his whole life outside, before he ended up there: school, the gym, friends. . . He saw himself smiling with the others and he thought that the Gabriel of that time would never have imagined ending up in prison.

Who knows what they were saying about him now? He envisioned the atmosphere of chatter in the school hallways, people saying things like, "And to think he seemed like such a good kid. . . ." And after that, what was he going to do once he got out of there? How could he look people in the face? How would he have behaved in their place with someone who had done what he had done?

The prison chaplain, a literally insane friar, had watched him for days and inquired about his story. Then he looked for the right moment to talk to him, to ask him, assuming he was Catholic, if he wanted to have Confession. Maybe then he would feel better. Gabriel had stared at him like he was an alien. Feel better? He was in jail –- no one knew for how long — he had killed someone so, as he saw it, his life was over. He hadn't even bothered to answer the friar. *This priest doesn't deserve an answer,* he thought. In the meantime, however, despair surrounded him and assailed him continuously. The only reason he did not give in to it was his promise to his mother. He was holding out for her because, even though he was in prison, he was not dead, and that, for his mother, was a consolation. She had already lost Michael, while he, on the other hand, was still here, even though he was a total failure, with no future left.

After the friar, the most unbearable thing was the new cellmate they had saddled him with after a week of being there. Gabriel really wanted to befriend him, but he had nothing to say to him.

"Listen, man," exploded the new comrade one fine day, fed up with all his attempts made, to no avail, up to that point. "We've been sleeping in this cell together for days and I haven't even figured out what your name is, so either you tell me or I start calling you 'thing.' I left you alone at first, to let you settle in, but it's already hard to be here; then, if I don't even talk to someone, I end up going completely crazy."

When Gabriel had given no sign that he had heard him, the guy sat down on his mattress without asking his permission. He was gigantic. . . Gabriel had to huddle up so as not to hit his head on the top bunk, which gave him enormous discomfort. The cot folded fearfully under this extra person's weight, causing Gabriel to roll toward him. Running away was not possible, and to fight did not seem to him to be the right thing to do. He did not want to worsen the situation. He was forced to sit down, to at least avoid touching that encroaching stranger. The cellmate took it for a sign that he was open, and began to talk about himself. His name was Richard, he was older than him by a few years. He had been in for a year and a half, for a history of dealing, stealing, and other such stuff, he explained vaguely. But all his life he had been in and out of foster homes and institutions, he recounted, as if that had been a badge of honor. His mother scraped by as best she could. He laughed incomprehensibly as he recounted it, but according to him she was the best woman in the world. His father, on the other hand. . .he could not even remember what he looked like.

"I am bad company, my friend," he commented, patting his jeans. "And don't think someone didn't try to help me. Lots of people have tried! The teachers at school, for example." He burst out laughing at some recollection. "I used to really give 'em hell, those ones! And then my mother and grandmother. But I'm not a very smart guy," he tapped a finger as thick as a sausage on his temple, "and in the end I didn't feel like working. It's not too bad here, come on. Free room and board and a nice roommate," he joked, patting him on the back.

Gabriel was horrified at the contact and turned his gaze incredulously toward him; was he an idiot or what?

Then he threw himself down again, showing this energetic guy his back, hoping he would take the hint, and pretended to sleep. He told himself that he was not like Richard. He would get out of there soon. Then he would face the difficulties outside but, in the meantime, to survive, he had to tell himself that this situation would not last much longer.

Six months after the fact, there had been no breakthrough and, indeed, things were getting worse and worse. The appeal against the rejection of the request for release, the revocation of the pre-trial measure, the request for house arrest – these had gotten nowhere. The lawyer told them that Matthew's family was hardpressed and aggrieved and wanted justice. "Justice!" Gabriel repeated to himself. This was gnawing at him; the right word was "revenge." They had not even accepted his apology and had even spoken of voluntary manslaughter, as some witnesses had reported hearing him say, "I'm going to kill you."

Gabriel did not remember saying that, but anything was possible, furious as he was at that moment. The lawyer was stalling. There seemed to be yet another issue: the fact that he was a boxer had aggravated the situation. The story of "The Iceman" had come out of who knows who, and the media had jumped on it.

Gabriel looked incredulously at his hands. The one he had hit Matthew with sometimes burned, and sometimes turned icy cold. If he could have, he would have torn it off. He was absolutely certain of one thing, though, and that was that he would never hit anyone again in his life, not even in the ring. He was horrified just by the idea.

Mom kept visiting him, encouraging him, giving him confidence, and perhaps she had noticed that he was losing hope. They both knew it took time, with the law and the trials, yet every day spent there was a day lost forever; wasted, flushed down the drain, Gabriel told himself. People outside lived, studied, loved, laughed, while he was forced to share a too-small cell with some kind of Neanderthal.

At first he took courage, telling himself he would get out soon, but instead he was still there. Guilt was giving way to anger and a sense of helplessness. He was a blister of frustration and regret about to burst.

"The women, over there," Richard told him one day, undeterred by Gabriel's indifference and searching for some topic that might interest him, "are freer than we are. They leave their cells open."

Gabriel squinted his eyes, considering this. It seemed incredible to him, who spent 23 hours a day locked in his cell, with outdoor "air time" being considered an hour of freedom.

"I highly doubt it," he commented.

Richard felt encouraged by his reaction and continued, "The friar told me."

The friar was the mad chaplain.

"He goes here and there. The females are quieter, he says. Fights break out here all the time, and so as not to have hassles, they keep us locked in. The friar also says that over there the women decorate *everything*! Cells, grates, bathrooms, kitchen. . . lace and ribbons everywhere!"

Hearing this tale, Gabriel unleashed a half-smile. It was probably the first time since he had been there that he had an expression other than a pout. Richard gave him a big pat on the back and laughed with him; the ice was finally broken.

Then what Gabriel could never have imagined happened: he got used to the place. It was horrible and smelled terrible and his body almost exploded from the forced immobility. His yard time was a heartbreak — the sky was always too small, sliced by the bars or limited by the impassable walls of the yard.

He took to going to Mass every day, because there wasn't much else to do, and although the friar continued to be unbearable, he was always happy, spouting optimism even in such a place, which, for the inmates, was magnetic. Besides, he made them laugh, and in one way or another he managed to get a smile out of Gabriel as well. In addition, the holy man began to supply him with a stack of books every week.

The first one he brought was *The Adventures of Pinocchio.*

"Are you kidding?! This's for children!" protested Gabriel.

"Read it," he replied.

Gabriel looked at the cover for a long time. He had no desire to read the book. He knew the broad strokes of its story and understood, because he was no dummy, that the friar had given it to him because Pinocchio was him, Gabriel, and frankly that didn't sit well with him at all.

He felt judged and it also seemed very unchristian of him. Eventually, however, boredom prevailed over pride and he read it. He finished it in one afternoon, being disturbed and moved by it.

"Well? What's wrong with you?" asked Richard, seeing him with that face and the closed book over his belly.

Gabriel did not answer and started reading all over again.

"If it's so good," Richard remarked after two days, fed up with having a fellow inmate who would sit quietly for hours reading, "why don't you read it to me?" Richard had never heard of Pinocchio.

Gabriel looked at him: why not? The third time, he read *Pinocchio* aloud, for Richard and those who wanted to listen. Strong, burly men with jail-faces stared at him open-mouthed and wide-eyed, as kindergartners would have done.

"Go ahead," they told him.

"Start again," they demanded when he was finished.

The second book the friar gave him was *The Betrothed*.

"I've already read it," was the response from Gabriel, who looked at the book wrinkling his nose. *Pinocchio* was better.

"Read it again, then. That's all I have for now."

"Do you know that priests should not tell lies?" teased Gabriel, reluctantly taking the book because he desperately needed to pass the time.

The new book was harder for his fellow prisoners to digest; too many descriptions, too many digressions, and old-fashioned, labored language.

That's when Gabriel set about narrating, cutting out the boring parts. The horrible, squalid death of Don Rodrigo, with the betrayal of Griso, made a great impression on the audience. The story of the Nameless One moved even the hardest hearts. Inmates talked about it at lunch as if the characters were real people, and took one or the other's side. One North African boy had even realized that their own chaplain friar was like Father Christopher in the book, and when he asked to see the "bread of forgiveness," the others mocked him, calling him an imbecile. In response, without flinching, the friar replied that he was going to fetch it. He returned after 10 minutes, with the stole around his neck and in his hand the golden monstrance with the host inside. Then everyone kept quiet because, as was often the case, he had won.

The third book that passed through Gabriel's hands was *Les Miserables*. He had never read it and his first thought was that it was remarkably thick but, fortunately, he did not lack time. And, indeed, as was to be expected, there too were endless digressions and minute descriptions, even of the sewers of Paris. Yet the friar knew his stuff, and the inmates easily identified with the truly overwrought affairs of convict Jean Valjean. They were moved by Fantine's death and cheered for little Cosette. Needless to say, they all hated Inspector Javert and reserved for him, in lunchtime conversations, the worst insults. It was an unusual and almost hilarious sight, hearing people like that talk about French literature or the Italian classics.

But the high point was Dante's *Inferno*. The ninth circle, of traitors, recounted by Gabriel flapping his arms as if they were Lucifer's wings, burned itself into the imagination of the audience.

At night, Gabriel would lie down on the bunk and take a long time to fall asleep. He thought about those outside, his classmates, the teachers. About the normal life they were living and the time he was wasting in there.

Tears of helpless rage would bath his face and fall onto the pillow. When those gloomy thoughts took hold of him, he would shut up like a clam and never want to speak again.

It was the friar, after the umpteenth of those gloomy nights and to avoid hearing any more of Richard's petulant complaints, who shook him. The man was reading him inside.

"What's wrong with you?" he asked, to prod him. But he knew very well what was wrong with him.

"I want to get out of here, pick up my life again."

The friar waited a while in silence, then resumed, "Why are you here?"

Gabriel became nervous, saying, "You know, why."

"Tell me again, I don't really remember."

Each telling required Gabriel to make a tremendous effort. But he had to accept it, because that was what had happened and there was no going back.

"I killed a person. By accident," he added.

"Yeah. So you can't leave just yet. Your life is here right now, and this is where you have to be."

"It was unfortunate. I had never beaten anyone outside the ring."

The friar did not respond.

"That's what you get for behaving yourself, all the time," Gabriel complained. "The one time you get out of line, look how your God fixes you. Stuck in here, in the dark, unable to see the sky; nice God indeed, yours."

The friar looked at him mysteriously. "What if this," he provoked him, "is not a leap into the dark as you think?"

Gabriel stared at him without understanding.

"You are a smart kid; change your perspective. You were in the dark before. This is a leap into the light."

"You, on the other hand, drank too much wine at Mass."

"You were in the dark and called it light. Now you are in the light, but you can't see because you are not used to it."

"I was not in the dark at all. Maybe I didn't have a perfect life, but anything is better than being here."

"And what do you know about that?"

The question was really too idiotic. That forced optimism served no purpose and, applied to his situation, only made people angry.

"I don't want to listen to you anymore," he raged, plugging his ears with his hands. But he could not escape; the friar's voice came muffled, but still reached him.

"Don't waste your time complaining. If you stay here, there will be a reason. If everything seems to have gone wrong so far, there will be a reason. Find out. We all have a job to do."

The friar left, placing a less-than-soft caress on his curly hair. Gabriel continued to hear his words for days. Was he there for a reason? Impossible. Beautiful God, the one who enjoyed putting him in there, stealing his time, taking away the best years of his life. But what God? There was no God, and if there was he didn't care about him, that was obvious. Otherwise, God would not have dumped him in prison for months. And after killing his brother. It was better to believe that there was no meaning, that things happened in the name of blind, irrational chance. One got less angry thinking this way.

For a few days, he even stopped reading to the other prisoners. He felt too angry. His mother had come other times. His father had sent his greetings, but he had not shown up. Gabriel did not mind; by now he understood and knew he was not mad at him. In the long hours of boredom, he could not help but reflect on the friar's words. After their last conversation, they had not spoken again. It's true, he had to admit to himself, the only thing I'm good for in here is to keep these people company with my books.

Stuff of paramount importance, in short. He didn't even understand why they were listening to him, much less why he was doing it. Simply to pass the time.

"Learning is easier said than done!" quipped Richard, who listened patiently to his daily outbursts. "This stuff, in ages of schooling, they've never been able to make me digest it! But the way you read it, I like it. And then I feel like I'm having big thoughts, which I never had before. Well, I feel better."

That last sentence unleashed a storm of thoughts in Gabriel's head. At 14 years old, he had chosen a classical high school track because he liked to study. There were a lot of things to learn and for him it was as Richard had just said: learning made him feel good, made him better. A light went on in his head. He resumed reading the novels aloud and went further, starting to entertain his fellow students by telling them about literature, history, and philosophy. He was surprised, even then, that those men listened to him and became so passionate about Orlando the Furious or the trial of Socrates. Meanwhile, the friar laughed under his mustache.

Ten years.

"That's the least sentence they could give you," the lawyer whispered to him, breathing a sigh of relief. He must have expected worse, although he clearly had not told him so.

But Gabriel, when the judge pronounced the sentence, almost fainted.

Ten years? In prison? That meant he would get out at almost 30 years old!

"Don't worry," the lawyer reassured him with a taut smile. "We're not stopping here. We will appeal."

"Don't worry? How could he not worry? Gabriel looked around, bewildered. He met his mother's gaze; her hope must have died too, and she was crying. His father, for the first time, reacted. He shouted, beside himself. The lawyer motioned for his mother to take him outside. There were people cheering; a distraught woman took to shouting at him:

"Murderer! Murderer! Serves you right!"

Gabriel looked at her fleetingly and immediately lowered his eyes as he realized it was Matthew's mother. He would have liked to apologize again, but he did not think it would help. She could not forgive him for what he had done. They forcibly removed the woman from the courtroom, and Gabriel was ushered out to be taken back to jail. He cast one last glance at his mother. She was no longer crying; in fact, she smiled at him.

But Gabriel cried the whole way back to the jail. He thought of Matthew's mother's rage-deformed face and was reminded of his own mother's composed one when she had been told that Michael had died. And the last look they had exchanged in the courtroom. "You promised," her steady eyes reminded him, "Don't despair." *At a time of disgrace like this*, Gabriel thought, *my mother smiled at me.*

He cried for two days straight. Richard cried with him, too, when he heard that the sentence had been so severe, because 10 years was really a long time.

"I'm an asshole and I deserve to be here, but you – you're a good guy. You're just a little bit of a loser."

"Don't talk like that," Gabriel told him, wiping away his tears, "and don't say 'just a little bit of a loser.'" Without knowing why, a half smile came across Gabriel's face. Perhaps, by virtue of listening to the friar, he was getting as crazy as he was.

If he did not go mad during those years, it was only because, as he had promised his mother, he never felt lonely. Richard was a friend, truer than those he had had outside. He was a simple, naive person, and perhaps, if he was there, it was not all his fault. He had attached himself to Gabriel, admiring the things he knew and the way he could say them, and his quiet manner. For a hothead like him, it was what was needed.

"When we get out of here," he told him one night from the top bunk, "I'm going to stick with you. Because me, without you, I'll be back in jail after a day. But with you close by, I bet I won't screw up again."

Gabriel smiled in the darkness.

Keeping his spirits up was the friar, with his unsinkable optimism. And finally, keeping him afloat, were the visits.

One of the first people to visit him, after the sentence, was his teacher, Mrs. Speranza. Gabriel at first could not believe his eyes.

"Mrs. Speranza!"

"Hello Gabriel."

He blushed. He was so ashamed to be seen there by her.

"They tell me that since you've been here, this is a different place." She smiled at him.

"Excuse me?"

"Father Francis is my friend," she revealed to him.

"Then you are the one who passes him the books for me!"

She laughed, but preferred not to elaborate. "Let's say we have the same taste."

"I screwed up, Mrs. Speranza." He felt the need to justify himself to her, and for that he felt like crying.

"Often, things don't go the way we want them to and certain consequences are unpredictable. You were very unlucky, Gabriel. Yet, I think we can do something good in whatever place or situation we find ourselves."

Gabriel was stunned to hear those words; they sounded very much like the words the friar had said to him and that had made him both furious and thoughtful at the same time.

"It's easy for people on the outside to talk like that," he dared to object.

"Do you think that doesn't apply to everyone? Do you remember Jacob, your classmate?"

"Of course, Mr. Nice Guy. How could I forget him?" bitterly remarked Gabriel, thinking that now that he had dropped out, Jacob must have become the best in the class.

"Yeah. He was discovered to have blood cancer. He's in the hospital, and there's no telling if he'll make it."

Gabriel stared at her in silence.

"His jail is an illness, and from that he cannot escape. In a nutshell, he is a prisoner in a hospital bed."

Is it better to be healthy and in here, Gabriel wondered, or doomed to die of a blood disease in a cancer ward?

She read his mind.

"What I want to tell you is that we are all prisoners. In here, you can be as free as – and maybe more than – those on the outside. No one but you can stop your thoughts, your dreams. Even in jail you can be happy and free, and useful to others. And here you can even dream, make plans; you can find meaning, have a goal. It's up to you."

Gabriel disagreed. It seemed to him that all those people who could roam freely and come and go as they pleased were making it sound a little too easy. Dreaming and being happy in here at the moment did not seem possible to him.

"Do you remember Horace?"

"Of course; he said you have to change the soul, not the sky. You used to tell us that in class when we were restless and complained about everything."

Gabriel was silent for a while, ruminating on that phrase. They were just the words of a guy who had died centuries earlier, and he had never believed they could have the profound meaning that gripped him now. Changing souls in a place where the sky couldn't be changed; it was always that, checkered, and hardly visible. He passed an arm over his eyes.

"Thank you, Mrs. Speranza."

"It wasn't anything."

"No, on the contrary, it meant everything."

Finally, his father began to visit him, although he usually kept quiet. From the outside, he looked like a tough, controlled person, and grief had made him even more withdrawn, but by now Gabriel seemed to understand him. And Mom, always so sweet and patient, was proving more and more every day to be a rock, an inexhaustible reservoir of trust and hope.

"We will try again, Gabriel. We will find a way. We will find a meaning to everything that is happening to you."

The most shocking visit occurred on Easter.

Staying inside when the scent of spring came in through the window was a daily torture.

"There is someone here for you," Frank, the warden, told him as he accompanied him to the meeting room. When he was Gabriel's age, Frank had wanted to be a painter, but, instead, had ended up, as a free man, working in a jail. Yet he never complained, and he often stopped to chat with Gabriel. In a strange way, they were friends.

"Who is it?" asked Gabriel as he followed him.

"Surprise. . ." he said, mysteriously. "But first, fix your hair."

When the door opened, Gabriel's first reaction was an irresistible urge to flee. He blushed tremendously and his ears were set on fire.

"Hello, Gabe."

"Hello, Jenny." Gabriel sat down in front of her.

"Sorry I came. I wanted so much to see you again."

Was she apologizing for coming? She wanted to see him again? Did she know what he had done? Wasn't she afraid of him?

"My mother brought me; she's outside."

Of course, Jenny's mother had not trusted her to come on her own. *Wise woman*, thought Gabriel. Her beautiful daughter with a convicted murderer; anyone would have hesitated. Gabriel fell silent with downcast eyes, unable to look her in the face. He wished he could read her thoughts; he racked his brain for the real reason she had come there. He could not think of a single one. Besides, he was ashamed to the core for what he had said to her, that distant morning a long time ago, when she had defended him in class. Instead, it was she who was apologizing for being there.

"Jenny. . .please forgive me."

"For what?"

Gabriel finally looked at her face, amazed; was it possible that she didn't remember?

"For the bad name I called you that time in school."

He was so embarrassed. Jenny smiled and a fantastic dimple popped up on the part of her face that had been spared from the fire.

"I had really forgotten about it!" She smiled again, gorgeous.

"Okay, sorry anyway. I was such a jerk."

Jenny laughed and the conversation blossomed. The bare walls disappeared and Gabriel, inexplicably, relaxed. They did not have much time to be together, and he decided that he would enjoy that little bit to the fullest. They began to talk about school, books, and even Jacob, and then Jenny's face became sad.

"I went to see him in the hospital, you know? He's in such bad shape," she told him, starting to cry.

Gabriel brushed her hands resting on the table, lightly, afraid that she would reject that contact. But Jenny took his hand between hers.

She stared straight into his eyes, piercing, entering his mind.

"There is a plan for everyone's life. I have understood that by now."

Finally, Gabriel understood why Jenny had come; she wanted to tell him that truth. Up to that moment, they had been talking about this and that, waiting for the right moment to bring it up. Jenny rotated her face, shamelessly showing the scar in all its ugliness.

"Do you think I never asked myself why this happened to me?"

Gabriel could not take his eyes off the scar, even though he knew it was terribly rude to stare at it with such insistence. Jenny smiled at him, not at all offended.

"And what answer did you give yourself?" he asked her with a dry mouth.

"The physical pain at first and then the daily pain of being stared at by everyone, with curiosity, or sorrow, or disgust, that was. . . Well, I'm a different person now. Better than the fool I used to be, when I spent my days putting on makeup, buying clothes, posting crazy pictures of myself and feeling very cool, better than so many others. And you know what?"

He shook his head no, taken aback by such frankness.

"I'm better off now. If guys don't want me anymore, it means that before they only wanted me because of my physical appearance. I am fine with myself now. I can be on my own and I don't care what others think or say."

Gabriel was dumbfounded.

"I mean," Jenny lowered her eyes, "what you think matters to me, but it's only because you're the smartest, brightest guy I know," she admitted, blushing.

Gabriel regained his voice and tried to hide behind sarcasm.

"Indeed, you can see how far my intelligence has taken me. . ."

Jenny smiled; his irony was what she liked best about him. "I guess intelligence doesn't have much to do with it here," she said with a laugh.

"Yeah," Gabriel admitted, "it's just bad luck."

"Anyway, you're doing something right here too, I hear," she winked at him, mischievous.

Mrs. Speranza must have told her about the books. Gabriel blushed.

"And it couldn't have been any other way, because you are you!"

Gabriel felt a pang in his heart, but he did not have the courage to ask her what she meant. Besides, the time for their meeting was already over.

"Can I write to you sometime?" Jenny asked him.

"If only!" exclaimed Gabriel. "If there's one thing I don't lack, it's time to answer you!"

When they were both out of earshot, Luca winked at him and asked, "Is she your girlfriend?"

"No," Gabriel replied without thinking. "Not yet."

He spent days thinking about Jenny, going over, word for word, what she had said. The pessimistic part of himself suggested that she had come to him the way she had visited Jacob, just because she felt sorry for him or because she had a crusader syndrome. But, in reality, he felt that the real reason was something else. Her compliments were sincere. He sensed her admiration for him and her affection, even though they seemed unbelievable to him. She had not asked him anything about what had happened the night of the accident. And it was not out of politeness; Gabriel would have bet on it. He could see from her eyes that she trusted him, that she seemed to know him and to know that he was not one to go around killing people. He felt a tingling sensation down his body – could Jenny really love him? Was there anything to dream about and to look forward to, outside of this place?

"So, wait for me, and don't make trouble until I get out!" he said to Richard as they hugged each other. They had spent a lot of time together, had become close friends. *The days without him*, Gabriel thought, *will be even longer.*

"Trust my father," Gabriel advised him. "He's not as bad as he seems."

"What do I know? I never had a daddy!"

The enlightenment had come to Gabriel during a conversation with his father. He had told him about Richard and his fear that, once outside, he might get into trouble again. Both of them, without telling each other, had thought of Michael. There was another idea that had been rattling around in Gabriel's mind for a while, but he hadn't mentioned it to anyone yet. In the meantime, however, Richard needed attention, and his father had accepted the crazy proposal to take care of him. Richard had no real place to go back to, so he was going to live at their house for a while, staying in what had once been Michael's room, to see if he could keep out of trouble until Gabriel got out of jail, too.

"And then what do we do, you and I, outside?" asked Richard.

"Don't worry, I have something in mind."

It seemed crazy to him, and yet. . . He had studied a lot in these years, sociology, psychology, criminology, law, statistics. And one night he had woken up all sweaty and with a wild idea in his head. An absurdly grand idea, unrealizable, and therefore perfect for him. A challenge from which it was impossible to escape. He wanted to seize it at all costs, because it was exactly what he had been searching for over the years, waiting for him to realize.

"Dad, you have to help me."

Gabriel had asked to have a meeting with his father. The end of his sentence was approaching; it was not long before he would be released from prison, and Gabriel was no longer looking forward to it.

In those years, his father had aged so much; keeping all the pain inside had accelerated the process. However, the experiment with Richard had gone well and now Gabriel had his own proposal to make to him. He was sure that his father could be reborn, just like him, if he agreed to follow him down this road, which no one had ever traveled.

"I have a project in mind, but I need you to help me."

His father did not say a word, did not blink.

"I've already talked about it with Mom, with Father Francis, with Mrs. Speranza, with a social worker, lawyers, and so on. In less than a year, I'm out." His eyes twinkled with excitement. "I want to organize a . . . net. A kind of last chance for the kids who are 'untreatable.' Those for whom neither parents nor school nor society think they can do anything anymore. If all seems lost to the rest of the world, I want to find a way to try to fish them out, to save them and give them another chance, like a new point of view, a new start, a dream."

He was thinking of Richard, of course. And of the many he had met in prison during those years. Some had been too fragile and had taken their own lives, some had come to a bad end as soon as they got out of there or had committed new crimes and were soon seen again with another sentence. Many of them were little more than kids, just like he was when they had thrown him in there. Action had to be taken before prison, before it was too late.

That was the point. That's why he had ended up in prison. It had taken him years to understand it. Although the method had been a little extreme, a tad too impactful, Gabriel had understood why he had come into the world. All those years, the best years of his life according to most people, he had spent in jail. Yet now he no longer felt like he had wasted them, and he knew that the ones ahead of him could really become the best ones, the ones in which he would do something important.

"What do you say, will you help me?"

The father looked at his son: he had grown up, he had become a man. This man was one that his other son, Michael, had not been able to become – partly because of him, Michael, but partly because he, as a father, had not been able to understand and help him.

"Yes," he agreed without hesitation. "As long as I am also part of this net."

Gabriel looked straight into his face without shame. His father had accepted everything that had happened to him. And now Gabriel knew that even though he had suffered and had never let on about it, he loved him and did not judge him. Despite his brusque ways, he loved him. Gabriel also understood why his father had agreed almost without thinking, participating in this crazy, radical project: he would have the chance to try to save boys who were like Michael – difficult, elusive, misunderstood. And along with them he would also help their parents, who would not feel alone and abandoned, as he had been, helpless in the face of an increasingly distant and lost son or daughter.

"Thank you, Dad."

"Thank you, Gabriel."

PART FOUR

DANIEL, MAGDALENA, ELIJAH, GABRIEL

A new envelope had appeared on the table. Daniel had been looking at it for a good half hour, but he did not want to open it.

"Go ahead," Peter encouraged him, brusque as always, but Daniel hesitated. What would the stranger demand of him this time? He couldn't imagine.

He took the envelope and reluctantly opened it.

YOUR TIME HERE IS OVER.
THANK YOU.

Behind those words, the usual map. Again. That meant he had to leave.

He looked Peter in the eyes and he read his mind.

"But I don't want to leave here," he replied as if the old man had spoken, expecting him to say the same thing.

"And yet you will," he answered him dryly.

This man has no emotions, Daniel thought; he lowered his eyes and crumpled up the map. Then he angrily walked out of the cabin and went to the headland. He was furious, with Peter and also with himself, because he did not think he could have grown so attached to the old man. In fact, he had never thought he could become attached to anyone. He was not even able to say thank you, though he knew that was exactly what he should say to him. Peter was a total nutcase, there was no doubt about that, but Daniel felt that toughness was his wacky way of showing his affection. After all, the softness of his parents and teachers toward him had yielded poor results. He had remained deaf to everything. But the old man. . . He had smacked him around, whatever, but that was just one incident and it had been only at the beginning. Then they had found their own balance. Peter had taught him how to fish, how to overcome his fear of the water, and how to regain some dignity. If Daniel read two lines now, he could understand them. He could stop thinking of himself as a total idiot. Peter had made him feel, for the first time in his life, capable. And then he had made him look up and like what he had seen; he had given him the sky.

Eventually, he had to stop being an offended child and return to the shack. When he entered, as expected, he found Peter throwing things into a backpack.

"What are you doing?"

He thought he was leaving, too.

"You'll have to walk for three days. I'll pack you some stuff so you don't freeze and starve."

Daniel's blood froze; three days in the woods? Again?

He didn't care if he appeared to be behaving like a wimp, so he spoke, getting straight to the point.

"I'm not sleeping alone, three nights out there."

"You won't be alone," he replied succinctly, without pausing in what he was doing.

"Are you coming, too?" asked Daniel, trying not to give away his hope.

"Of course not. What do you take me for, your wet nurse?"

Daniel fell silent, offended. He wasn't going, alone, into the woods; it was out of the question.

"Look, you can't stay here anymore. Either you leave on your own, or I'll kick you out."

Daniel looked at him, more hurt than if he had been slapped. Did Peter really not care about him at all? Did he really not want him there anymore?

"I'm not the one who decides," he then added, in a neutral voice. "Didn't you understand that? I am not the boss. I obey."

Daniel's eyes widened: obey? Was that old curmudgeonly bully obeying someone? Peter interpreted his silence.

"We all obey someone. And you know what? Sometimes it's even restful, knowing that someone decides for you."

No, Daniel definitely did not like to obey; he wanted to do his own thing, even if there was a risk of making a mistake and getting hurt. Since he was in those woods, he had *had* to obey, or else they would let him starve! But out of there...

For the first time, he thought concretely about himself being out of there. What would he do? Would he go back to his former life? Maybe not.

"I'm not ready to go home," he found the courage to say to Peter who, meanwhile, ignoring his silence, had resumed minding his own business.

"Of course you're not ready," he replied, as if it were the most obvious thing in the world, but he added nothing more.

"So where am I going?" asked Daniel anxiously.

As was to be expected, Peter did not answer the question and merely communicated, "You're leaving in the morning."

Daniel lowered his head. There was no use arguing with him; he had learned this the hard way.

On their last evening together, Peter took him to the headland. The sky was exceedingly clear and the moon was casting an incredible light. In the city, with the streetlights, he never paid attention to the sky. It seemed impossible for Daniel to leave this sky for the other; this one was big, immense, freeing him with thoughts he didn't even know he had. The urban sky was invisible and empty.

"Even the stars obey." Peter broke the silence.

"How?" Daniel wasn't sure he understood correctly.

"Even the sun, the moon, and the stars obey. They are huge – you are less than an atom in comparison – yet they too submit to a higher law. The universe is order, and there is no order without law. Law is perfect harmony."

Daniel was used to his soliloquies and did not give them too much weight, partly because he never quite grasped them. He was grateful to Peter, though, because he addressed him as if he could understand, as if he took it for granted that he had a brain.

"Hey, are you listening to me?" The old man's voice pulled him from his musings.

"Yes, yes," he answered him quickly so as not to irritate him.

"You have to know who you are to obey. To obey does not mean to be weak, to submit. It means to be strong and confident. If you know how to obey, you will also know how to lead, but you have to choose the right leader to follow."

"I'm not really good at that," chuckled Daniel.

Peter became serious, with that lost, sorrowful expression that would show itself from time to time, along with the bad memories, probably. "Because you always take the easy way out."

Daniel did not understand, but Peter did not add anything else.

Even though the old man kept quiet, he sensed within Peter a kind of magma of bad thoughts in constant motion, a viscous substance that swelled and bubbled. Peter managed to quell it, as his emotions tried to boil up again. He felt Peter throw out all the rotten air in his body; saw him close his eyes and fill his lungs with oxygen and the serenity of the stars. Without opening his eyes again, as if seeing what he was talking about as he said it, Peter resumed speaking.

"I had a son, you know."

It could not have been at all easy to be his son, Daniel thought, but perhaps he would even have liked to be.

"He's dead."

Daniel noticed that his voice had not cracked; it had probably happened a long time before.

"He chose the wrong path and didn't take help or advice. He wanted to go all the way, but he didn't find what he was looking for."

Daniel did not know what to say. Grief and death leave one speechless; few have words, let alone him. He had never seen a real dead person, only in movies, and he didn't really have any idea what it was like to lose someone dear. He had almost drowned, though, and he remembered that all too well. He would have liked to know more about Peter's son, but the man stood up, as if to say that the talk was over. Peter, however, surprised him again, pressing his hand firmly on his head.

"In the end, remember, it is we who decide whether we are angels or beasts." And behind the serious marble face, Daniel sensed something like affection.

Daniel had his backpack on his shoulders and everything in him was screaming at him not to go. He was fine there, in those woods, with the crazy old man. He did not know what he would find at the X on the map and, whatever it was, he would not like it as much as the place where he was now – that he already knew.

"Bon voyage," Peter said, without another word, holding out his hand. Daniel squeezed it, trying not to cry. There was still that word pressing against his teeth that his pride would not let him say. He knew that if he held it in, he would regret it later. One ... two ... three...

"Thank you," he spat out in a low voice and bowed head.

Peter nodded and pushed him toward the door. He sent him out begrudgingly and closed the door behind him. Daniel felt terrible but, after all, that was how it had started between them and probably neither of them was very good with goodbyes or manners.

"Kitty!" he called, and his faithful fleecy cat popped up from around the corner of the shed. "It's off again."

At least in the woods he would not be completely alone. I wonder if it was Kitty that Peter was thinking of when he had told him he would have company. He doubted that, in case of an attack by wolves, bears, or aliens, the cat would be much help.

He yawned. He had slept little the previous night, due to restlessness and because the old man snored louder than usual. He marched for a good hour before sitting down to peek in his backpack. Who knows what he had put in it – it weighed like a sack of cement.

Finding the bird book in his hand he squinted. Once he would have been angry; what was he doing with a book? It was not like he could eat it! Instead that surprise filled him with a strange feeling, gratitude, perhaps. He put the volume back carefully and grabbed a sandwich. He checked: there were nine in all, three a day. That wasn't much; in fact, it was nothing for the chronic hunger he had. He gave up the sandwich and just drank the water. I know where to get more of that, if it runs out, he told himself as he heard the sound of the river not too far away. Kitty had disappeared, a few minutes before, and now he was coming back with a bird in his mouth. It was a small blackbird.

"You have to eat, too," he told him, even though he felt sorry for the bird. "Blackbirds are very intelligent birds," he explained to Kitty.

The cat looked at him funny, with his one eye, feathers sticking out of his mouth. Not so smart, if he got caught by me, he seemed to tell him. Daniel petted him, then went on his way again.

THANK YOU FOR WHAT YOU HAVE DONE.
YOUR TIME HERE IS CONCLUDED.

Waking up in the morning, Magdalena had found the sign and stood frozen in front of it. So? What was going to happen? Her heart leapt into her throat: perhaps her mysterious do-gooder would finally show up! Would he come for her? In any case, she had to get her act together. She washed and changed her clothes, ran her hands through her hair several times to untangle the knots, ate dinner, and lay on her bed, daydreaming. She had to leave her sheep and Shep, but she would see the stranger. What was he going to do? She could see herself jumping on him and then, perhaps, to thank him, she would kiss him. She would have to play it by ear, seeing how he would react to the embrace. She struggled so hard to get to sleep; in the morning, she would be exhausted.

Shep woke her with a lick to her face. On the table was a backpack. Magdalena went to open it. Inside there was food and water, as well as breakfast and a map.

"He wants me to join him," she explained to Shep, who looked at her adoringly, wagging his tail.

After stuffing the ribbon into her backpack, she went out, desperately hoping to find the stranger outside, waiting for her. She shrugged, stretched, and went to say goodbye to the sheep. But the stable was empty, and Magdalena was heartbroken. Then she recovered; at least the dog stayed with her!

"Come on, Shep, let's go." Following the map, she set out, driven by a desire to finally meet the mysterious man who had been taking care of her all that time.

The woods were fragrant and the birds were flitting about. She walked, putting all her effort into it, eating when she felt hungry. Her backpack was overflowing with food, enough for an army – it was the stranger's way of showing her that he cared about her. On the map was marked how far she had to walk each day. It took three to reach X, passing the place where she had grazed her sheep. Perhaps, by walking more expeditiously, it might have taken even less time, but she trusted him and obeyed.

When night fell, she did as she had seen in the movies. She gathered some wood, made a circle with stones and, with the lighter that was in her backpack, she built a fire. Spending the night there alone might have been terrifying to her. What nocturnal animals lived there? Wild boars, perhaps. Foxes. Maybe bears? Well, she had no idea and didn't care to find out, either. Fortunately, Shep gave her security, even though he was a wimp of a dog. But she was sure he would keep watch and wake her up in case of danger. Leaning her back against a tree, she dined, sharing her food with the dog. With each crunch she winced because of the noise of her chewing and, from time to time, Shep would start growling in some direction, his teeth bared and his ears straight. Or he would turn away, go sniffing around, and then return to her.

"He would never put me in danger," Magdalena reassured herself loudly. "Right, Shep?"

Repeating those words to herself like a chant, she finally fell asleep.

The first night passed horribly.

"I knew it, I knew it," Daniel hissed between his teeth.

This time, he made a fire and there was Kitty to keep him company, and food and a blanket, but that was not enough, so he had to put on spare clothes as well. The night in the woods was worse than a nightmare. Noises everywhere, above, below. . . Creaking and the usual damn owl that had almost caused him to die of a heart attack, making him wake up with the feeling that they were killing a woman. The darkness made everything scary, although his brain tried to reassure him with credible arguments. Kitty was hardly a guard dog, and all of a sudden the coward had even climbed a tree. Daniel had almost chickened out. Who knows what he had heard? Elijah came to his mind and he wondered what had happened to him. At that thought, Daniel shuddered.

Dawn came, as always, too late. Half-frozen, Daniel resumed walking, his mood even darker than black. By mid-afternoon, when the fear of the impending night was already assailing him again, Kitty leapt up like a spring and climbed the nearest tree. Out of a bush came a barking black and white dog, not very big but frightening. Fearing it would bite him, Daniel picked up a stick and lifted it threateningly.

"Don't even try to touch my dog," a female voice said.

Daniel looked up into the eyes of . . . a girl. His jaw dropped and his mouth opened in surprise.

"Shep, come here," the girl resolutely called to the dog, who obeyed. They slowly approached each other, studying one another.

"I am Magdalena." She held out her hand to him, confident as she had learned to be.

Daniel shook her hand, hiding his agitation behind the old tough guy mask, summoned from who knows where.

"What are you doing here?" she asked, casually.

"The same thing that you're doing here, I guess." Daniel was unfazed.

Magdalena showed him the map. They compared them; they were leading to the same destination.

"If you want, you can come with me," Daniel proposed, playing it cool. He was actually overjoyed that he was no longer alone.

"Whatever," replied Magdalena with a shrug.

Daniel didn't let on that he was offended by Magdalena's apparent indifference. In one gesture, to make an impression, he slipped off his sweatshirt, which would have gotten in his way anyway, showing a tank top now reduced to a rag; he hoped with all his might that she didn't mind and instead noticed how muscular and tanned his arms had become by dint of hard labor.

"Wait, I'll get my cat back." And praying to the gods that they wouldn't make him look bad, he began to climb up to retrieve Kitty, who either didn't know or didn't want to come down anymore. Meanwhile, out of the corner of his eye, he tried to observe her reaction. But Magdalena seemed not to care at all and had crouched down to talk to the dog.

When Daniel was at the top of the tree, Kitty flew into his arms and climbed up, scratching him on his shoulder and then on his head. Daniel felt foolish with that fur headgear, but he knew from experience that it was useless to try to shake him off. He was about to lower himself down, when he stopped, petrified.

"Well?" asked Magdalena from below.

Daniel waved her off and pointed to an invisible spot among the branches. His eyes glittered. He remained silent, watching the hoopoe standing guard, ready to fly away.

The stupid dog barked, and the bird opened its wings and flew away, in a swish of white, brown, red and black.

"Did you see it?! Did you see it?!" he asked Magdalena excitedly, once he was back on his feet.

"Yes, what was that thing?" she asked with little interest.

"It wasn't a thing! It was a hoopoe!"

Magdalena did not flinch. "So what?" said her face with condescension.

"I've been waiting weeks to see it! If it wasn't for your stupid dog. . ."

"Well? You've seen her now, haven't you? And my dog is smarter than you."

"You wouldn't understand."

They resumed walking, needling each other, and so the road seemed to both of them shorter and less strenuous. It was nice to have company after all the time spent without talking to anyone, even if the girl didn't quite understand him and looked at him as if he were a strange being, or so it seemed to Daniel; all the fault of that silly cat who had taken his head for a pillow. Daniel didn't take the cat off his head, though. After all, he made Magdalena laugh and Daniel was playing the sympathy card, since he didn't currently have any other angle.

"What happened to your cat?" she asked him, reaching out to pet him.

Daniel handed it to her for her to hold and set about making a fire for the night, mentally praying not to make a bad impression with that, too. The wood slowly caught fire.

"He's been through a lot, like me," he explained to her.

It was a phrase said on purpose to force her to ask a few questions, but Magdalena kept quiet. They ate their sandwiches in silence, staring into the fire. The night was not scary between the two of them, and it also seemed less cold. They had stopped teasing each other, and a strange atmosphere was developing between them. Since Magdalena was not taking the initiative,

Daniel began to talk about himself, how he lived before being abandoned there, the crazy things that had happened to him, his meeting with Elijah, who had disappeared into thin air, and how he felt at that moment. He had never spoken so much, much less to a girl. But all those months in the woods had changed him. All his life, he had been ashamed of himself and, having no alternative, had been forced to brag about his faults, always behaving at his worst. Now, however, he was beginning to like himself and was desperate to tell someone.

"What about you?" he asked Magdalena, having concluded his soliloquy.

Magdalena was not at all certain that she wanted to tell that stranger about herself. She did not feel proud of her past, although she had begun to accept it. She mentioned to him her problems with food, and Daniel looked at her in a way that flattered her. It was clear that he did not find her fat or ugly at all. Then she told him about gymnastics and showed him the ribbon, but she refused to perform in front of him. "I'm not fully back in shape yet," she apologized.

"It doesn't look like it to me," Daniel replied, getting a resounding, grateful smile all to himself.

They were tired, neither of them feeling like acting; there was no need for it there. The dirty, faded clothes, the shaggy hair – it was impossible to pretend to be someone else in that condition. In the end, they were honest with each other, as can happen only rarely, in abnormal situations, when all defenses fall. In the dark, in the middle of a forest, with a stranger who has much more in common with you than you think.

They slept close enough together, with the dog to Magdalena's right and the cat in the middle, for her not to escape again. When they woke up, Shep was gone. Magdalena called for him for a long time, but he didn't show up.

"Where on earth could he have gone?"

"You said it; he's smarter than I am. He'll find us again, you'll see."

Unconvinced, Magdalena agreed to set out again.

"According to the map, we have arrived," announced Daniel. It was amazing to him that he had walked through a forest for three days, following a map, and managed to arrive alive at his destination. "The X must be around here."

They had stopped in front of a wall of brambles clearly not marked on the map. It must have been right between them and the destination. Daniel, who wanted to impress Magdalena, refusing to accept her stubborn indifference from the day before, chose the tallest tree and climbed with agility. He did not take off his sweatshirt this time; he felt like an idiot for having done so when they had first met. What a chump he had been!

His heart began to beat fast; beyond the thick wall of brambles, amidst the trees, a roof could be glimpsed.

"There's a house!" he shouted, turning to Magdalena. "A real house!"

No shacks! he thought, relieved. Maybe there was even a bathroom. And a shower.

From the little he could see, it looked like a picture-perfect mountain cabin. Climbing down from the tree, Daniel looked around for a passage to reach it. It didn't take much exploring. Out of a gap in the thorns, half-hidden by the tall grass, barked Shep. He leapt into Magdalena's arms, covering her with drool. Daniel bent down and saw that there was some kind of narrow burrow through the hedge. Okay, that was to be the last test; Daniel braced himself for the fact that he would come out covered in scratches and wearing nothing but the tatters of what little was already left of his clothes. He looked for a stick and widened the passage; Shep let go of Magdalena and disappeared back into it. Daniel crawled in first. Shep came and licked his face.

"Go away, you stupid dog." He tried to send him away and continue on.

"Don't insult my dog," came Magdalena's voice from the mouth of the tunnel, but he could hear she was joking.

The passage was so narrow that Daniel could not even turn around.

"I'm coming in, too," the girl's voice came, over-fatigued, from behind him. "Let's get a move on; this narrow space makes me nervous."

Eventually, they reached the exit and stood again. Daniel could not see himself, but he was sure he looked terrible. Magdalena sidled up next to him, pulling the sleeve of her sweatshirt over her hand and running it over his cheek.

"You are covered in blood," she whispered. Then she added, "Thank you for going first."

Daniel shrugged, to indicate it had been nothing.

They looked at the house as they approached. It was wooden, with geraniums on the windowsills and curtains on the windows. *Never seen a house like that*, Daniel thought, comparing it to the peeling apartment building he lived in with his parents. With a knot in his throat, he knocked at the door.

"There's no one there," Magdalena said, disappointed.

"Maybe they can't hear," said Daniel and, looking up, he noticed a rope hanging from above, attached to a cowbell.

They rang it forcefully. Finally, there was movement on the other side; someone was fumbling with the handle.

"Welcome."

Daniel and Magdalena gasped. The stranger's welcoming smile had something disconcerting about it, and the way she looked at them — it seemed as if she had known them all their lives.

"Daniel, Magdalena, it's a pleasure to have you here. Come on in," she invited them.

She moved to the side, clearing the passage, and they both couldn't help but notice the scar that marred the right side of her neck and face. It was especially noticeable since, with that short haircut, she was doing nothing to hide it. She did not seem at all embarrassed by their gaze. Their impression was confirmed as she arranged a strand behind her ear, making everything more visible.

"I am Jenny. Gabriel is not home yet. Meanwhile, I'll show you to your rooms."

More than a little confused, Daniel and Magdalena followed her. Who was she? How did she know their names and why was she treating them so familiarly? Also, what were they doing there and what was the point of the whole thing? It had started out in a preposterous way, and on it went.

Jenny opened a door, showing the inside of a room with two beds.

"'Magdalena, if you don't mind, you will share the room with Nina. She's over there in her study now; I'll introduce her to you later. In the meantime, you can take a shower. There are clean clothes in the closet." She smiled at her, as if she knew exactly what she needed. "Then go back through the hallway and wait in the dining room. Daniel, you can come with me."

Daniel and Magdalena exchanged a fleeting glance; they knew each other very little, yet they both felt they would rather not part at that moment.

"Let's go." Jenny walked off and Daniel reluctantly followed her, waving goodbye to Magdalena and trying not to let it show that he was sorry to leave her.

The room was too obsessively tidy for his taste. He also could not help noticing that there were, unfortunately, two beds.

"If you don't mind, Daniel, you'll share the room with Philip."

What if I do mind? thought Daniel. Would he get a single in that case? He looked at the made-up bed, perfectly smooth, and thought maybe he would find it too comfortable and not be able to sleep in it.

"You too can take a shower," Jenny suggested to him.

Daniel was sure he was not giving off a good odor, although at least it was no worse than the one emanating from Peter, who in fact had never complained about it. Besides, his face was flayed by brambles and he could feel his skin pulling from congealed blood.

"I guess you have to be a little patient, though," Jenny advised him, smiling. "Philip is in the bathroom."

Now who the hell is this Philip? thought Daniel.

227

"You can do the introductions yourself," she joked. "I'll be here for you when you're done." And she left him there.

Daniel stood listening in the silence to the sinister noises coming from the bathroom. They were not very reassuring; there were dry thumps, a suspicious trampling, and someone talking to himself. Daniel seemed to distinguish a few swear words as well. He waited and waited, but it was going on and on. He went around the room, trying to figure out which bed was his so he could throw himself on it and not have to wait on his feet for the boy in there to be finished. Finally, the door opened.

"And who the hell are you?" was the welcome from a young boy in a wheelchair. "Oh, right, you're Daniel, the one who was supposed to come."

Daniel did not answer; the stench coming from the bathroom caused him to gag. Philip noticed and immediately huffed. "Well, do *you* smell like cologne? I don't think so. In fact, see that you take a shower. You smell like 10 goats."

Daniel made an effort to ignore him and opened his backpack to get his clean clothes.

"There are new clothes in the closet," Philip told him acidly. "But see that you don't touch mine. And the beds, both mine and yours, need to be perfectly made. The creases and the disorder give me anxiety and I get into a fit."

Daniel looked up at the scrappy little boy. He had a ridiculous face, with glasses that exaggeratedly enlarged his eyes and a horrible Superman haircut. Someone like that was anything but super. And his bossy ways clashed with everything else.

"What's the matter? Don't you understand me? Are you deaf?"

Okay, thought Daniel, making an effort at self-control that once would have been unthinkable for him. *Whoever had put them in the room together was definitely in the mood for a joke.* First he was alone, then with the crazy old man, and now with this moron. Daniel felt an irrepressible urge to escape welling up in his limbs.

"So, are you going to move or not? What's the matter, are you retarded?"

Being called retarded by that kid on two wheels immediately turned his mood around. He grabbed some random laundry, deliberately threw the stuff that was in his backpack on the bed in disarray, and his dirty clothes on the floor. *Have all the fits you want, dude,* he thought to himself, and walked into the bathroom.

The air was unbreathable, so he opened the window. Then he dove into the shower. It was the most wonderful thing in the world; abundant hot water coming out by simply turning a knob. He closed his eyes and enjoyed the feeling of pure pleasure. When he opened his eyes again he let out a cry.

"What the f---?"

Philip was staring at him through the glass.

"First of all, the windows must be closed," he informed him. "You must not waste water. Also, you can't swear here, if you haven't been told yet."

"Didn't they also tell you that you shouldn't look at people while they're showering?" replied Daniel to him, thrown off balance.

He had only known him for five minutes and he already felt like he wanted to kill him.

"Beat it, Wheels."

"And didn't they tell you that handicapped people should be treated well?"

Daniel hurriedly dried himself and got dressed, ignoring the obnoxious jerk. He wanted to get back as soon as possible to Magdalena, and also to Jenny, to tell her that it was all right for him to sleep even in the basement, or on the yard in front of the house, or on top of the roof, as long as it wasn't with Wheels.

"Wait for me!" Philip chased him down the hall. "You haven't even put away your stuff!"

Daniel sped up and closed all the doors behind him, to put as much time and space as he could between himself and that competitive pain in the ass. He arrived in the dining room. Only Jenny was there, reading a book.

"So, have you met Philip?"

Daniel remained silent.

"I know he's a little difficult, but you'll get used to him. You'll see how nice he can be."

"I don't think so," Daniel said mournfully, "and I don't want to room with him."

Jenny totally ignored him, as if she had not even heard him, just as the old man always did. *Where is Magdalena?* wondered Daniel through a veil of despair. *I wonder if she had fared better with her roommate.* Certainly she was still in the shower; women are terrible when it comes to the bathroom.

Nina must surely be a child. Her stuff, in the closet, was all strictly pink and small in size. There were no toys in the room, though, only pictures. Lots of them. Magdalena quickly passed her gaze over them, eager first of all to take a shower. It took her a long time; she enjoyed every drop of water, brushed her hair for a long time, looking in the mirror at her new image, rounded, feminine, definitely beautiful. She wanted to be perfect for when he arrived. Gabriel, Jenny had said. Maybe that was his name.

When she was dry, she looked at the paintings more carefully. They were small, but meticulous in every detail; they were mostly imaginary landscapes with mesmerizing charm.

"What do you think?"

A little voice behind her made her jerk. She turned around and stood before a bizarre creature of all colors.

"What, you've never seen a dwarf?" said Nina in a joking tone.

"Actually, no," replied Magdalena, still amazed.

"Well, there's always a first time," she replied in a matter-of-fact tone, disappearing into the bathroom to wash off the paint she had scattered all over herself.

Magdalena joined the others in the dining room. She noticed Daniel staring at her with an incomprehensible look, but she did not understand what he wanted to tell her. Perhaps he, too, had had a strange encounter in his own room.

"Later, Gabriel will tell you the rules of this place. For now, you can take a tour if you like. As soon as the bell rings, it's time for dinner."

Daniel didn't let this be repeated twice; he grabbed Magdalena by the arm and left the house with her before Wheels found a way to open the door he had blocked with a chair.

"Okay." At Daniel's horror-comedic account of the shower peeper, Magdalena burst out laughing. "I have no idea what we are to do here, but I assure you that even I can hardly believe what I saw," and she told him about Nina and her 10-foot ego. "She made an impression on me, that one — I can't imagine having to share a room with her."

"I, on the other hand, never thought I'd miss the old man," Daniel said, lying, trying to get out something to make her laugh. "Anyway, it was worse for me."

The sound of the bell echoed like thunder in the silence of the woods to call them back to dinner. Magdalena's stomach clenched at the thought that she would finally meet Gabriel. She quickened her pace.

"Hey, how hungry are you?" laughed Daniel, struggling to keep up with her.

They were all sitting around the set table. The smell coming from the kitchen was not exactly the most inviting. The door opened and a very large man entered.

"Sorry I'm late," he mumbled.

Magdalena was taken aback; he was too old and very unattractive. He looked like a child imprisoned in an adult's body – clumsy, awkward, and even a little stupid.

"Come, Richard," Jenny invited him, smiling at him.

Magdalena breathed a sigh of relief. Jenny introduced her and Daniel to the giant.

"Hello, folks!" he greeted the newcomers as if they already knew each other. "Gabriel is coming," he added as he looked at Jenny and jumped into his seat.

The door opened again and Gabriel entered.

He was as Magdalena seemed to remember him: tall, slender, with a face that showed no emotion. Only when he leaned over Jenny and kissed her on the neck, right on the scar, did his face look for an instant like someone else's, transfigured by joy. *That must be the face people make when they meet an angel*, Magdalena thought.

That gesture, so intimate and full of meaning, which she couldn't grasp, threw her into despair. How had she not thought about it? How had she ignored the ring Jenny had on her finger, identical to the one she now noticed on Gabriel's hand? They were married. And he would never look at her because, how could he deny it, disfigured Jenny was still a million times more beautiful than she was. And not because she was thin and tall, but because there was something about her that made her irresistible. But Magdalena could not grasp what it was.

Gabriel, instantly becoming serious again, turned to Magdalena and Daniel and welcomed them. "Before we get down to dinner, it is necessary for me to explain the rules of this place. There are fixed hours and activities, which Jenny may have already explained to you. But most importantly..." he raised his hand in the air, pointing with his finger to an inscription above the door.

LOVE AND DO WHAT YOU WANT.

Nice! thought Daniel, focusing only on the second part of the sentence; exactly what he liked to do all along.

"Love." Magdalena had tears in her eyes. Love who? Love how? She did not know how to love, or at any rate she always loved the wrong person.

"And now," he concluded, "let's thank Daniel for this food." Daniel looked at him questioningly, suspecting she was teasing him.

"'Oh yes!" smiled Jenny. "Cabbage dinner!"

Was that his cabbage? Daniel couldn't believe it, disregarding the fact that he had never eaten it in his life, because of the bad smell it was known to give off once cooked.

"Cabbage soup," Nina announced, pushing a cart into the room. "Sautéed cabbage with toasted bread and fried cabbage. Bon appétit!"

The others set about eating. As she chewed, Magdalena, out of the corner of her eye, looked at Gabriel to see if he was pleased with her. He just ate; it was Richard who winked at her and mouthed, "Good job!" and added a thumbs-up. Daniel was still staring at the plate. Jenny noticed this.

"I know it doesn't' look good. I'm not exactly a good cook."

"Neither am I," Nina quipped, not at all sorry. "Tonight was my turn to cook, but cabbage doesn't inspire me much. I generally don't have much imagination in the kitchen. With paint brushes, yes. However, with cabbage. . ." She paused for effect. "Not to mention that I can't even reach the stove!" she teased.

Magdalena envied her for the self-confidence that exuded from every pore. If she were in her place, she would not even leave the house.

"Well?" Philip piped up in his nasal voice. "If you don't eat it, I'll take it." And he made to stretch his fork into Daniel's plate.

At that point he woke up, protected his plate from the attacker, and heroically swallowed the first spoonful. It smelled unclean, like the bathroom after Philip's passage, but the taste was bearable. The rest, all in all, he liked and even cleaned the plate with the bread.

"Magdalena, you can go to the kitchen and take care of the dishes. Daniel clear the table, please," Jenny asked at the end of the meal.

She was so endearing in her mannerisms that Daniel did not hesitate a second to obey, especially since Magdalena had already sprung to her feet and he did not want to be outdone. He picked up the dishes and took them to the kitchen, where Magdalena was the dishwasher. For the tablecloth, he was forced to accept Philip's help.

"Will you get a move on, you slowpoke?" Philip provoked. "Looks like you've never folded a tablecloth in your life."

Daniel was ready to respond in kind, but a voice beat him to it.

"You still haven't learned how to be nice, have you, Philip?"

It was Gabriel, with the worst of expressions on his face. Philip immediately lowered his eyes.

"Come on, you know the rules: thank you, sorry, and please."

"Sorry, Daniel," he muttered between his teeth.

"Okay." Daniel preferred to get out of there, taking the tablecloth from the little boy's hands and going straight to the kitchen. "And thank you!" he said to Philip, certainly not to please Gabriel, but to spite him. It was possible that he liked Gabriel even less than Philip.

Jenny asked him to sweep and mop the floor, which Daniel clumsily did, while Philip took revenge on him by running his wheels over the still-wet tiles.

"Can we go to bed now?" asked Daniel, gruffly addressing Jenny. He was was fed up with Philip always getting in the way.

"Sure."

"Then I'll come too," said Philip immediately.

Daniel wanted to throw himself out the window. Or throw Philip out. But they were on the first floor.

As expected, as soon as they got to their room, Philip was unbearable. He demanded to use the bathroom first and left it a mess. He also "accidentally" used Daniel's toothbrush and took half an hour to find a comfortable position in bed. In the middle of the night, he woke Daniel up by throwing a shoe at his face. Then he fell into a state of deep sleep in three seconds flat, snoring so loudly that Daniel could not fall asleep until dawn.

By seven o'clock he was already in the kitchen complaining to Jenny: it was either him or Philip.

"One more night together and we'll be dead," he threatened grimly.

Jenny turned to him and smiled amiably with her eyes.

"Maybe you didn't understand," she told him gently. "It is you who must help him."

"Me?" Daniel fell silent. He had never expected that.

"Of course. Philip is a spoiled and stubborn little boy. I think being with you will only do him good."

Yes but, the thing is, I don't want to help him, Daniel thought, but he didn't have the heart to tell Jenny. He couldn't explain why, but he was concerned about making a fool of himself with her. "Can I hit him, at least?" he wanted to ask her, because as soon as he saw Philip's face he felt his hands wanting to reach out and smack him.

Jenny announced that he would have to clean their room with Philip that morning, and then study together. Dress rehearsal for hell, in short.

"Look, Wheels," Daniel quipped bluntly, "you pissed outside of the toilet; you clean it up."

The bathroom smelled worse than an outhouse.

"Listen you, you retard," Philip answered him in turn, "I'm in a wheelchair, so I don't clean a damn thing. And don't call me Wheels."

They went on arguing for a good half hour, but the bathroom wouldn't get cleaned by the barrage of insults.

"Do you know that if we don't work, we won't get lunch?" Daniel tried to reason with him. It was his last attempt before smacking him around.

"*You* don't eat. I'm in a wheelchair and they have to give *me* lunch!"

"Why?" retorted Daniel angrily. "If you pass out from hunger, you're still sitting." He felt really witty.

"Ha ha ha," pretended Philip in amusement. "You know, you really make me laugh. Get a move on, I said."

"Okay," said Daniel exasperatedly, and like a demon he began to unmake the beds, his and Philip's, throwing pillows and sheets into the air. Then he remade his perfectly and left the other with only the mattress. "My side of the room is taken care of. You take care of yours."

Seeing his bed in disarray like that, Philip turned red and began to shout.

Maybe he wanted to get the others' attention, but Daniel didn't give a damn. They were welcome to come and see what an idiot he was.

"I'm in a wheelchair! I can't do anything!" screeched Philip, screaming and shaking himself all over like an epileptic.

Daniel was not impressed in the least and stood looking straight at him with his arms folded and a defiant smile on his face. The scene lasted a good 20 minutes until Philip, exhausted, pretended to faint. At that point, Daniel couldn't take it anymore and burst out laughing.

After a minute, Philip was still slumped in his chair. Daniel waited again, then the doubt came to him that perhaps he had really fainted. He walked over to him and brought his own face close to Philip's, when the boy raised his head sharply.

"Asshole!" he shouted sneeringly.

Daniel, seriously feeling like an asshole, gave the wheelchair a push and walked out of the room. He wished he could have smashed him against the ceiling with an uppercut.

He went to the kitchen in search of Magdalena. Instead, he found Jenny.

"How is it going?" she asked him.

"Lousy. One more minute and. . ."

"So you give up?" she teased him subtly.

Daniel did not like those words. "No way," he heard himself say.

"Then go."

"Yes." Jenny had set him up. "I'm going now," and he returned to Philip.

Daniel entered the room and found that Philip had also thrown his bed up in the air, and was now watching him waiting for his reaction.

"So you know how to unmake the bed," he told him, with a patience he didn't even know he had, "but you don't know how to make it again."

"Yeah," the stubborn boy answered him, with his usual smug face.

"And the reason is that you're in a wheelchair, right?"

"Right," he confirmed, satisfied because even the retard had gotten there in the end.

"Right. Get out," he signaled him to move out of the wheelchair and onto a chair.

"Huh?" Philip looked at him incredulously from behind the thick lenses of his glasses.

"Come on, get out."

He didn't know how he had come up with this crazy idea, but at least Philip would have no more excuses. Philip suspected nothing and believed him. With Daniel's help and leveraging his arms, he moved to sit on the chair in front of the desk. Daniel took his place in the wheelchair and began to move around the room. Every now and then he would mismeasure and bump on an edge.

"Clumsy," Philip teased him, but always with less conviction.

Eventually Daniel made both beds, cleaned the bathroom, and even started doing wheelies in the wheelchair.

"See? See? You too can do everything in this chair!"

Philip was dumb with rage.

"Give it back," he shouted to him, red with frustration, dangerously flailing all over in the desk chair.

Daniel became serious and helped him back into the wheelchair.

"You can get up whenever you want," said Philip, offended. "Too easy, like that."

Daniel did not know what to say anymore and left the room, closing the door; he was not so sure he had won.

"But who is she?"

Magdalena did not know where to look, in that room scented with tempera and oil paints and with the walls covered with drawings. Then her eyes landed on a painting of a life-size girl. Nina looked at it with a strange smile.

"Come on, tell me who she is," insisted Magdalena. She wished she was as beautiful as the girl portrayed.

"Can't you see it?" asked Nina with her plump hands planted on her hips, firm on her stubby legs. She held her in suspense for a while, then replied, "That's me!"

Magdalena was sorry to disappoint her by telling her that there was no way that six-foot tall girl was her at all. Perhaps Nina was missing a cog, despite the incredible images that came out of her head, which her brushes then executed beautifully. From the way Magdalena looked at her, with a mixture of compassion and superiority, Nina understood what she was not saying. She did not mind at all.

"You see what you want to see," she explained to her without smiling. "But I dreamed of myself one night. And I assure you that I am like that inside."

Magdalena had confirmation: okay, she was missing a few neurons.

"You, on the other hand," Nina resumed, "you see yourself as beautiful, tall, attractive. . ."

Magdalena wished she could have told her that she struggled every day with herself to convince herself that she was as Nina had said.

"But actually. . ." The dwarf grabbed a sheet of paper and sketched something on it with a charcoal pencil. The speed of her fingers was inversely proportional to their length – their agility was impressive. Magdalena watched her drawing quickly, with her tongue between her teeth and a wrinkle in her forehead. "But really . . . you, inside . . . are like this." She turned the paper over: there was a likeness portrait of Magdalena, indeed, a caricature of her with the features of a dwarf. She did not like that joke at all.

"Yeah," said Nina with profound insight, "inside you are still small and deformed."

"That's not true!" Magdalena would have liked to shout, but she could not take her eyes off her portrait and the picture . . . of Nina's soul. She burst into tears.

Yes, it was true; she had always worried about the outside, but in the end she was a wooden puppet, hollow on the inside. Nina took a bench and put it next to her, climbed on top of it and passed an arm more or less around her shoulders.

"Up . . . up," she comforted her with pats on her back. "For the outside you can do little, but with the inside you can work. I said 'still small and deformed,' didn't I?"

If I have to take lessons from a dwarf, thought Magdalena. . . But, deep down, she felt Nina had spoken the truth.

"Is it true that you stayed back three times?" Philip asked Daniel, and at first he did not understand whether it was an innocent question or the usual attack. Knowing him, however, the latter was more likely.

The topic didn't phase him anymore; he felt a little less of a numbskull after Peter's "cure." Still, to avoid any more harm, he didn't answer him. He had learned not to get sucked in by his barbs, and if that wasn't an accomplishment. . . .

"Yes or no?" he insisted.

"Yes," Daniel tried to shut him up once and for all.

"Ha ha ha! So you are retarded in every sense of the word," he humiliated him.

"Do you know what a magpie is?" he was surprised to ask him, instead of insulting him back as he deserved.

"Of course, it's a bird." Philip was not unprepared.

"No. It is the most obnoxious of all the birds. It's lazy and doesn't know how to nest, or maybe it doesn't feel like it. So, it waits for other birds to leave their own nests and goes in and lays its eggs and makes itself at home there."

"So what?"

"You are just as obnoxious as a magpie. Now, let's study."

He had never tried so hard in his life. Philip was a junior in high school and was two years younger than him. Daniel's job was to explain the lesson to him. Too bad he didn't know it himself, so he had to read it carefully first and then repeat it back to him. And besides that, it was practically impossible to concentrate with that horsefly, who was constantly prodding him and laughing at him. At the end of each explanation, Philip would look at him silently for a long time and then say, "I didn't understand." Every time. By the third time he repeated the lesson, Daniel had changed the sentences in so many ways that he thought he had been crystal clear. But Philip invariably repeated, "I didn't understand."

"Then that means you are the retard," Daniel finally offended him, at the height of exasperation.

They had been going on with that little dance for a week. *Ugh*, why was he wasting his time with it? Why was he agreeing to commit himself every day to this impossible task? He was sure Philip understood perfectly — he just didn't want to give him satisfaction.

"Or maybe," he taunted him, "it's that, as a teacher, you really suck." He closed the book impatiently and threw it in his face.

The reaction was instantaneous: Daniel slapped him in the face so hard his head spun the other way. In fact, Philip's glasses flew off, landing under the bed.

Then Daniel fled; he felt like a coward. He could not remember ever doing a nastier thing than that, except when he had seen his mother fall to the floor. Thinking about that made him feel even worse. In addition to the sharp but bearable pain in his nose from the book Philip had thrown at him, there was something else that gave him a twinge inside. *How had the teachers put up with me for so long? And I was far more irritating at school than Philip*, Daniel conceded in retrospect. He was not cut out to be a teacher, that was for sure. He was not cut out to do anything. Maybe at most he was good at digging rocks out of the ground and watering cabbage; stuff that didn't require great intelligence or special gifts.

He hid behind the house with his head in his hands. That was how Nina found him.

"Hey, I've been looking for you; it's your turn to help with lunch today."

Daniel looked at her. She was definitely ugly, and she mispronounced words, yet it was glaringly clear that even she was better than he was.

"I don't know if I'll eat today."

"Well, the rest of us have to eat, though. You can do whatever you want then," she told him in her matter-of-fact way.

Daniel laughed; it was impossible not to feel sympathy for that chick. It had only taken Magdalena a few days to change her mind, too, and now the two of them were spinning in love and agreement.

"Okay, but I don't know if they'll let me stay in this place."

As soon as he said it out loud, Daniel realized that he definitely wanted to stay.

"Your time here is not over," Nina said.

"I slapped Philip," he confessed, looking into her eyes to see her reaction.

They stared at each other in silence. Then Nina burst out laughing. "Ha ha ha! It's about time someone beat the crap out of him!"

Daniel put on his typical "Whaaaaat?!?!" face.

"Well, it's clear that Gabriel can't beat him up. He would never beat anyone. But it had to happen sooner or later. Not that violence is a good thing here or anywhere else. But when it's needed, it's needed."

Daniel immediately thought of Peter and how he had shaken him the time he had tried to eat what was not his to eat. He felt a little less bad. "Okay, I'll go to the kitchen then."

Nina nodded.

"Thank you," he told her, and he was surprised that it had not cost him any effort to utter those words.

In the kitchen, Jenny worked in silence, but it was clear that she already knew everything, who knows how. However, unexpectedly, she did not say anything to him. Perhaps she had agreed on this with Nina and, in any case, she knew perfectly well how Philip treated Daniel. *Only a saint would be able to restrain himself,* he thought.

At the table, Philip ate without saying a word. Daniel never looked up from his plate, for fear of seeing everyone else's eyes fixed on himself.

"The pasta with sauce is great," complimented Richard, filling his plate for the third time. "'Good job, Daniel."

"Yes, it is, thank you," said Magdalena. Since she had been there she was looking more serene, less sad.

"Good job," Gabriel said seriously, and then Daniel lifted his eyes and realized that maybe he wasn't just talking about the pasta.

"Will you tell me your secret?"

Nina looked at Magdalena as if she had been a rare animal. "If you teach me how to do that stuff with the ribbon," she asked in return.

Magdalena stared at her, questioningly.

"We watch you every night, me, Philip and Daniel, from their bedroom window."

"You spy on me, that is!" said Magdalena peevishly.

"Well, you practice on the lawn, not in a secret vault, so it's possible for someone to see you. It's very nice. Will you teach me, then?"

Magdalena measured Nina with her gaze. In spite of everything, she was sure that with the ribbon in her hand she would amaze her, as only she could do. She was always full of surprises.

"Okay," she agreed, "but first you have to tell me your secret."

Nina seemed to think about it for a while; she didn't seem to know where to start.

"How old do you think I am?"

Magdalena thought about it intensely.

"I don't know. . ." It was really hard to say. "Maybe 18. . . 20?"

"Thirty-one," Nina astounded her. "And two degrees: one in fine arts and one in psychology."

Magdalena gasped.

"Plus a degree in the conservatory," Nina dropped the final bombshell. "So I think, at 31, if you keep working at it like you're doing, you'll be a confident woman, too."

They remained in silence, looking at each other and, rarest of all, Nina smiled. Magdalena, recovering from her surprise, burst out laughing.

"Thank you, Nina, you are unique!"

"Yes, I know."

After the slap incident, an icy air hung between Daniel and Philip. They rarely exchanged a word. Each focused on his own part of the room, as if the other was not there. *This*, Daniel thought, *was only because Philip was so proud and stubborn that he was unable to apologize.* He was the one who had thrown the book in his face, he was the one who had to apologize. Daniel had no intention of humiliating himself to take the first step.

Daniel did not feel sorry for Philip; he just got on his nerves.

Then, one night, Daniel was awakened by a strange noise, a kind of choked breathing. It sounded like someone was crying in the dark. He remained silent, wondering if he was dreaming. In the darkness he could not distinguish much; perhaps Philip was having a dream, and he turned on the light to check. Philip was not in his bed. He was on the floor, his dry, skinny legs stretched out in front of him. Perhaps he had fallen off the mattress and could not get up. In any case, Daniel did not intend to offer him help; he already knew what he would say to him. They looked at each other for a very brief moment, then, perhaps reading his hesitation in his face, with a mean expression, Philip growled at him, "Fuck you."

"Suit yourself." Daniel turned away, shoving his head under his pillow and trying to get back to sleep. For a moment, the absurd idea had even crossed his mind to help him. If Philip wanted to catch pneumonia, it was certainly none of his business.

The next morning, Philip acted as if nothing had happened. Someone must have come in the night to put him back in his bed. Daniel, as he was wont to do, did not ask too many questions. But two nights later, the scene was identical. Philip was on the floor again. This time, big tears were falling down, wetting his face, and with his arm he was wiping snot from his nose. It was a pitiful scene, and Daniel just wanted to sleep.

"What's wrong with you?" he finally asked him, exasperated.

"'Magdalena. . .'" sobbed Philip.

"Huh?"

"Have you seen how beautiful she is?"

"Yes, she is beautiful, but now go to sleep," Daniel cut him off. This did not seem to be the right time to talk about such things, and the two of them were certainly not friends.

"She will never like me. She may like you because you're muscular and you walk. I suck. I disgust myself. I want to be like you, I want to *be* you!"

Those words had the power to melt something in Daniel's chest. Perhaps, for the first time in his life, he felt something akin to compassion. In his underwear and t-shirt he got out of bed and, effortlessly, like an older brother, grabbed Philip from under his armpits and hoisted him into bed.

"Everyone is the way they are. Some of it is destiny, some of it is us deciding what we want to be."

He realized that this was the lesson he had learned from Peter.

"There is little to complain about. We make our own destiny," he concluded.

If those who had known him before the whole thing heard what he just said, they would have gone wild with surprise.

"I didn't pick these sticks." Philip smacked his legs in annoyance.

"Okay. But you don't have to focus on what you can't do. You need to find what only you can do, what you're good at."

"And what am I good at?"

Daniel racked his brain for something encouraging to say, but found nothing. "Busting my balls!" he joked.

Philip did not expect this and burst out laughing.

"I don't know what you're good at," Daniel added, turning serious again. "You have yet to find out."

Philip wiped his eyes with the sheet.

"And by the way, Magdalena doesn't even look at me," Daniel added defiantly. "I think she has a crush on Gabriel."

Some females were very good at always slipping into the most far-fetched relationships, and in Magdalena's case it was really a shame, because she was a knockout and Daniel dreamed of her, eyes closed or open, two nights out of three.

"You're too dumb for her," commented Philip, but he could tell he was joking. "Sometimes it's not even enough to be beautiful," he remarked.

"Then what are you whining about at 3 a.m.?" Daniel gave him a pillow before turning off the light. "Go to sleep. Good night." He resumed sleep immediately, with a strange peace in his heart.

It had been a long time since Daniel and Magdalena had arrived at this place, and things were really starting to settle. One evening, they were at dinner; it had been Magdalena's turn to cook. They were eating and talking like a bizarre but sincerely happy family.

Suddenly, Jenny froze, her gaze fixed outside the window and her spoon in midair.

"What is it?" asked Gabriel, immediately alert.

"Nothing," replied Jenny. "I thought I saw something out there. I was mistaken."

A chill ran through them all. They started eating again, but no one felt like talking anymore.

"Oh my God!" cried Magdalena a few moments later, and Philip, in fright, dropped his fork to the floor.

Magdalena pointed with a trembling finger to the darkness beyond the glass.

"There is someone outside. I saw eyes."

Everyone fell silent, and the look of apprehension that Richard and Gabriel exchanged froze Daniel's blood. Although they had not said a word to each other, he feared he knew to whom the eyes Magdalena had seen in the dark belonged.

"He found us." Gabriel confirmed his thoughts, turning to Richard. "Stay here," Gabriel ordered, and he and Richard got up from the table and went outside.

They could have cut the tension with a knife. Daniel disobeyed and followed them. Jenny, who was trying to calm Philip and Magdalena down, did not notice. Gabriel and Richard had closed the door behind them but, without making a sound, Daniel held it ajar and looked out.

It was dark, the silhouette blurred in the darkness, but Daniel still knew it was Elijah. He had become almost unrecognizable, much more like an animal than a human being. His clothes were in tatters and showed more than they should; he no longer had shoes on and had grown skinny, a bundle of muscles. It was eerie to see him like this, almost naked but still wearing the cap he had stolen. Daniel heard a strange noise, a kind of low, continuous growl. He shuddered when he realized it was coming from Elijah.

"Come here," Gabriel told him, keeping some distance away, but reaching out toward him gently so as not to alarm him. His voice was firm and resounded in the silence of the night.

Daniel realized that he had almost stopped breathing, standing behind the door, waiting for what would happen. In Gabriel's place, he would have chickened out. Richard, a short distance away, also looked petrified, but Daniel imagined that, if need be, he would have sprung very quickly to Gabriel's aid. Or at least, he really hoped so.

"Come," Gabriel repeated again, moving half a step closer to Elijah, who responded to those words with a frightening guttural sound, as if he had forgotten how to speak.

Where has he been all this time? How did he survive? wondered Daniel. He had not bent to any rules and was now little more than an animal. "And do you want to be angel or beast?" Peter's words rang in his ears. Daniel was certainly not an angel, but he had not become a beast, either, even though he had been at risk to become so. He opened the crack in the door a little more to get a better look. Gabriel sensed movement behind him and became distracted. Elijah, with the instinct of a wild animal, took advantage of that instant to pounce on him. Gabriel dodged and, like a true boxer, hit him in the ear, but without force, only to shrug him off. Richard had also sprung, but Gabriel signaled him with his arm not to approach and stay where he was.

"I don't want to hurt you," he reassured Elijah.

The boy seemed unable to understand. Frothing at the mouth and with bloodshot eyes, he returned to approach, more angrily than before.

"Elijah," Gabriel called him by name. "Elijah. . ."

A glimmer of humanity passed through Elijah's crazed eyes, which froze for a moment.

"Elijah," insisted Gabriel. "Come to your senses."

Elijah lowered his head like a tame dog, but when he was close enough to Gabriel, he bared his teeth and bit at the arm that was held out to him. At that point, Richard was quick to intervene, hitting Elijah hard on the neck, and the latter slumped over, unconscious. Gabriel's arm was bleeding profusely. Daniel noticed that his own legs were shaking with fear.

"Daniel! I know you are there," Gabriel's voice called out, quiet and steady. "Tell Jenny to call an ambulance."

Daniel complied and moved away, with difficulty. With his powerful hands, Richard barely managed to force open Elijah's jaws, which were still clamped around Gabriel's arm like the sharp points of a box cutter.

"Can you go get Gabriel, please? The doctor is here," Jenny asked him. Daniel did so, deeply troubled.

He still felt shaken about what had happened. The ambulance had arrived and Elijah was strapped to the stretcher and hoisted onto the vehicle. At that moment, he had regained consciousness and had begun to struggle and scream like a maniac. They had to sedate him. It was a horrible sight.

Following the drops of blood on the floor, Daniel stopped in front of a door. He was normally not allowed to open it. However, following his instincts, he silently opened it without knocking, searching the room.

Gabriel was kneeling on the floor, sobbing. It was the first time Daniel had seen such an intense expression on his face. Usually he seemed balanced and detached from everything but now, he was upset. He watched him as his shoulders shuddered in despair and his fists balled into his eyes, looking like a little boy. Daniel didn't understand.

"Why? Why?" repeated Gabriel on the floor.

Daniel stepped back, closed the door, and knocked.

"Come in" came Gabriel's voice after a while, firm again but very tired.

"The doctor is here," Daniel reported.

"Thank you, Daniel, I'm coming now."

But he did not move. Daniel wanted to ask, even at the cost of being scolded for spying; he needed to understand.

"Why were you crying like that? Does your arm hurt?"

Gabriel stared at him; his eyes seemed to dig into his gaze, able to see inside him. He didn't answer right away, but got up from the ground and walked over to him.

"I can't give myself peace about Elijah, Daniel."

"But he is the one who chose."

"I know. And he tried to take you with him, where he was going. And you also chose – not to follow him. He had been given a new chance and he turned it down."

"You did what you could. In the end, what part did you play?"

Gabriel fell silent. He stared him straight in the eyes.

"We always have something to do with it. All of us."

"You can't force others to choose to be angels," Daniel heard himself say, as if it were someone else speaking.

"My father taught you that lesson very well." And he smiled at him in a way that shocked him. He had the same expression as Peter. And just as Peter had once done to him, Gabriel pressed a hand to his head, like a father to a son.

"I thank you, Daniel." Then he walked past him and left him alone in the room.

Daniel awoke with a sense of foreboding. There was a yellow envelope with his name on it above the desk. He did not need to open it to know what it said.

YOUR TIME HERE IS OVER.
EXCELLENT WORK. THANK YOU.

He knew it would be completely useless to try to protest. He had learned his lesson and needed to make room for the next person. He went to the kitchen and found Gabriel there. A simple "thank you" was not enough this time to express all his gratitude. And if he was Peter's son, he knew he would not know how to do anything but shake his hand. They stood looking at each other in the deserted kitchen, with the ticking of the clock marking time.

"I'm very proud of you," Gabriel said simply, his eyes shining with satisfaction.

Tears started to well up in Daniel's eyes and he did not stop them, because if someone like Gabriel had cried, that implied there was nothing untoward in doing so.

"I don't know if I'm ready to leave," he managed to say, because that doubt was pressing in his brain and chest.

"Every day you have to decide who you want to be; it is not enough to have chosen once and for all. Falling back into one's mistakes is easy. We must be brave men to love ourselves as we are and walk the path we have chosen."

"What about Magdalena?"

Daniel wanted to keep seeing her, once they were out of there. Something had been born between them, he was sure. It was only in its budding state, but it had great potential, he could feel it.

"She is not ready yet. She needs a little more time," Gabriel replied dryly. "Go say goodbye to whoever you have to and get your backpack; your father and mother are outside waiting for you."

With his heart in his throat, Daniel went. Philip was in the bathroom, as indicated by the empty bed and the ever-present swearing that came, muffled, from behind the door. *Dealing with even the most mundane things in daily life is a constant challenge for him*, Daniel thought. That little boy had much more courage than he had realized at first.

When Philip came out, disheveled and in a bad mood, Daniel smiled at him.

"Philip, I'm leaving."

Surprisingly, a quivering pout appeared on the boy's face.

"I'll leave you something, though. . ."

He had thought about it and could not take it with him. Kitty was a wild cat; he would go crazy within the four walls of his apartment. Not to mention he wasn't sure his parents would let him keep him. He opened the window and called him over, and Kitty immediately leapt onto the windowsill, as if he had been standing guard all night out there.

"Here." Daniel took the cat and handed it to Philip. "'He's yours."

The somewhat less stray life he had led in recent times, that is, since he had arrived at Jenny and Gabriel's house with Daniel, had made him less gaunt. His fur had grown back, thicker and shinier. For the eye and the ear there was nothing to be done, and yet Philip had always liked that creature, too, for the same reason

Daniel had taken it with him: he was imperfect, exactly like them, and yet, for that very reason, unique. And the pieces he was missing were part of his story.

"Bye, then," Daniel said.

He picked up his backpack and threw in it the only three things he cared about: the book on birds, the ruined shoes he had repaired himself, and the compass, so he would never get lost again.

He could not leave without saying goodbye to Magdalena.

Although it was not usually allowed, he went to the girls' hallway. He knocked and entered. Nina was at her desk, probably awake since dawn.

"I'm going," he whispered to her.

Magdalena moved in the bed.

"Be good, then," Nina told him without smiling.

"Thanks for your advice. . ."

"Do you want a last kiss?" And without waiting for an answer, she pointed with her head at Magdalena and put her hand to her heart in a very funny gesture.

Daniel turned purple. Nina ducked into the bathroom to make it easier for him to approach. Magdalena meanwhile had awakened and pulled herself up in bed, resting her head on one arm. With her hair uncombed and her eyes still clouded by the dream she was having, Daniel found her irresistible. Without giving it too much thought, he knelt beside the bed, exactly like the prince in an illustration he had seen as a child in a kindergarten book. He thought that there had never been anything fairy-tale-like in his stories with girls.

"Are you going away?" Magdalena asked him with bated breath, seeing his backpack and understanding on the fly.

She could not stay there without him; she had always thought that they had arrived together and together they would have to leave.

"Yes, but I promise I'll be good until you get out too. And then I'll come find you."

What was he saying? What kind of cheesy movie had he gotten himself into? Yet he felt it was all true.

"That is, if you want me to," he added quickly, for perhaps he had taken certain things too much for granted.

Magdalena clung to his neck, bursting into tears. She knew it was right, but that didn't have to make her like the way things were going. She felt that she was not ready, that there was still that part of wood in her that needed to become real flesh.

Yet, Daniel waited until she had calmed down.

"Bye, then," he broke away. Their faces were very close. "See you soon."

He got up and walked to the door. Nina's suggestion was a good one, but in the end he had not found the courage. He turned to cast one last glance at Magdalena, to imprint her well in his empty head, whose memory was always too short. Magdalena was sitting cross-legged on the bed and stared at him as if he was abandoning her.

He didn't kiss me, she thought, confused. She wasn't used to guys who didn't immediately go for it all. Instead, Daniel's behavior was telling her that he liked her, but he would wait, because now he had learned to wait. She realized only at the moment of parting that he was the one she wanted. And that pending kiss between

them would be the thread that would hold them together until the next time they met. Like a promise to
be kept.

She waved goodbye and Daniel walked out. He felt
like a fool and a hero at the same time. He returned to
the kitchen.

"Say goodbye for me to Jenny and Richard," he said
to Gabriel.

"Yes, they don't like goodbyes very much," he ac-
knowledged. "Neither do I."

He held out his hand and Daniel shook it, in silent
thanks.

"Now go," Gabriel urged him.

Daniel shuddered, feeling himself unexpectedly
overcome by a kind of joyful longing to see his parents
again. Gabriel opened the door for him and there they
were, with the same old beat-up car and anxiety in their
eyes. Mom, however, was smiling, as in that faded photo
from when he was a child that he had been staring at for
days. Daniel walked down the steps and joined them.
He turned to say goodbye to Gabriel one last time, but
he had already closed the door.

A WORD OF THANKS

Thank you (in strict chronological order):

To my dad, who was my first teacher of humor and writing.

To my mother, for being as simple and generous as Jenny.

To Alberto, who attempted the first brave submission and continues to support me, in any way he can.

To Maria Serra, who bet on my stories first.

To Lucia Bacci, an unwitting instrument of the DP.

To Antonella Boldrini, of the spade club, for the catalyzing idea for this story.

To Giuditta Boscagli, for the sincerity with which she told her incredible story of love . . . *Jailbird*, from which I was greatly inspired.

To Nicola Mucci, for the legal advice.

To Father Angelo for the imprimatur and to Father Francis for the inspiration.

To Fabrizio Altieri, for introducing me to Chiara Pullici.

To Chiara Pullici, for taking over this story and making it . . . levitate.

To Marco Erba, for his friendship, advice, and uncommon helpfulness.

To Valeria Riboli, for her valuable, patient work.